OUT *of* TIME

Paula Martinac

D0064212

Seal Press

Seal Press
3131 Western Avenue, Suite 410
Seattle, WA 98121
sealprss@scn.org

This book is a work of fiction. Although names of actual historical places and people appear, the events described are fictitious. Any resemblance to actual people or events is coincidental.

Series design: Patrick David Barber
Cover design: Lee Damsky
Cover photograph (top right): E. O. Hoppé/Corbis
Cover photograph (middle left): Ken O'Brien Collection/Corbis
Author photograph: Katie Hogan

Library of Congress Cataloging-in-Publication Data
Martinac, Paula, 1954–
Out of time / Paula Martinac.
I. Title.
PS3563.A729809   1990   813'.54-dc20   90-36973

Printed in the United States of America
First Djuna Books edition, March 1999

10   9   8   7   6   5   4   3   2   1

Distributed to the trade by Publishers Group West
In Canada: Publishers Group West Canada, Toronto
In the U.K. and Europe: Airlift Book Company, Middlesex, England
In Australia: Banyan Tree Book Distributors, Kent Town, South Australia

Acknowledgements

My thanks go to the following people for their help at various stages in the writing of this novel: the women of the Lesbian Herstory Archives in New York City, particularly Deb Edel, for helping me locate source material on lesbians in the 1920's and Judith Schwartz for her inspiring book, *Radical Feminists of Heterodoxy: Greenwich Village, 1912-1940*; Suzanne Seay, for her meticulous typing and retyping of the manuscript, for catching all those embarrassing inconsistencies, and for her encouragement and support; Maureen Brady for a thoughtful reading at a transitional stage; and Barbara Wilson and Faith Conlon of Seal Press for the time they took to help me shape this book. I am also grateful to the friends whose hospitality gave me a change of scene and made the revising process easier: Pete and Barbara Seay in Guilford, Connecticut, and Nancy Kraybill in Venice, California.

"Quite suddenly, some moment of the past has become totally real, as real as the present, and we realize that it is as real as the present—or rather, that the present does not have some special status of super-reality, just because it happens to be here and now."

Colin Wilson, *Afterlife*

◆ 1 ◆

For a long time, I forgot the date that I walked into the antiques shop, but now I remember it again. For months, I was not even sure which shop it was. I could see the inside clearly—the floor-to-ceiling bookshelves lining one wall, the homey scattering of bric-a-brac over creamy lace doilies, the black silk evening gown trimmed with jet beads draped casually across a velvet-upholstered settee. But when I tried to find it again, I always ended up in the wrong place, with concerned salesclerks asking if I was looking for something in particular. No, I answered, because I was not sure what I was looking for, or what I thought I would find by being in the shop again. I ended up apologizing to them for my confusion and standing helplessly out on the sidewalk, looking north and south, and wondering if it was Sixth Avenue I was on that day and not Eighth.

I remember that it was raining and that I ducked into the shop just as the rain started to drip off my hair onto my cheeks. I shook my head like a dog as I stepped through the door. A bell tinkled as it closed behind me, and I noticed with embarrassment that I was dripping onto a small Persian rug. At the sound of the bell, the shopkeeper had appeared through a damask curtain at the back of the store.

"Don't worry," she said, seeming to understand why I wasn't budging from the entry. "It's just water."

I smiled and began to move around carefully. I was the only customer in the shop, and each creak of the floorboards under my feet resounded through the room. The shop looked more like a middle-class parlor in 1910 than a store. I took in everything but touched nothing, afraid of intruding. I wanted to be out on the street again, or in another shop where I would be less conspicuous, where I could happily browse through the merchandise, feeling like a customer and not a house guest. But how could I leave without appearing rude?

The shopkeeper said, "Feel free to pick things up," again reading my mind. "Antiques should be touched, picked up, lived with." She smiled from behind the counter, where she was carefully rearranging a tray of marcasite pins on a deep red velvet cloth. Her fingers were long and delicate and they seemed to embrace each pin as she touched it.

I cleared my throat and said, "Thank you," but it came out hoarsely. I realized they were the first words I had spoken in several hours.

I gradually made my way to the bookshelves, once or twice lifting an object from a table to inspect it, but less out of interest than out of a feeling of obligation. I was more comfortable at the bookshelves, my eyes scanning the titles quickly, zooming in on the interesting ones. I was always looking for the same thing, and every now and then I found it. Once I located an old copy of Radclyffe Hall's *The Well of Loneliness*; in another store with shelves of old paperbacks, I found several lesbian pulp novels from the fifties, including Vin Packer's famous *Spring Fire*. It had been inscribed on the title page, "To my Charlotte, you set me on fire, Yours forever, Jeannie."

I had a small shelf in my apartment for these books. It wasn't really a hobby yet, maybe just a passing phase that I would someday look back on and say, "Oh, yes, that's when I was buying old books about lesbians." I never read them, I just stacked them on the shelf. More than being interested in the books, I was fascinated by trying to imagine the women who had owned them, who read and reread them, who dog-eared the pages, who dusted them every week, whose fingerprints oiled the pages and whose tears made circles on the paper. When I held the books, it was almost like holding the women, protecting them from the silence of time.

Because it wasn't a real hobby yet, I didn't know exactly what to look for. I didn't know the titles I should be hunting, beyond the most obvious ones, and I must have passed over a lot of valuable books because the titles were vague. I tended to look at anything with the word "woman" in it, which was usually not very fruitful. I had a few authors' names, like Helen Hull and Jo Sinclair, but I almost never found anything written by them.

So mostly it was luck. And that day I remember I had almost turned away from the bookshelves. I was thinking of looking at the pins, because I needed a present for Catherine's birthday. I thought I had spent a reasonable amount of time shopping, so that leaving wouldn't be rude. And just as I was turning, my eye caught an oversized green Moroccan leather book on the table next to the bookshelves, which looked as if it had just been tossed there. On the cover in gold leaf was stamped the word "Scrapbook."

I had a scrapbook of my own, which I had been saving for posterity. Someday, I thought, it would be scrutinized by curious, hungry lesbian historians. The scrapbook was a chronicle of my first relationship, with Elaine Loring, and was pasted together when I was a romantic teenager. It included everything from movie stubs to pressed roses to the program from my senior prom, where Elaine and I were the dates of the Calabrese twins, Rob and Rich, who later moved to San Francisco and opened a gay nightclub together.

So I flipped open the cover. Inside it was more of a photo album than a scrapbook. It was similar to an old album my mother kept, with little black paper mounting corners holding the photos loosely in place. Half of the corners had lost their glue and were gathered in the binding, falling out as the pages turned. But in this album, there were no pictures of Mom and Dad or uncles, aunts and cousins. I flicked the pages over quickly, taking in the faces of four amazing women.

The first pages held photos of the group of them, in various poses and locales. They were labeled on the borders, "The Gang at Montauk" or "The Gang at Provincetown." "The Gang," it appeared, traveled a lot. Then there were the winter season shots, The Gang members in fur-trimmed coats with cloche hats pulled tightly down to their eyes, which peered out at me seductively. None of the group pictures were labeled with names, and I felt cheated. I turned the pages more quickly, till I came to a section devoted to Harriet. Harriet in a high-necked white lace blouse, in the purity of girlhood. Harriet in a low-waisted mesh dress that just grazed her knees. Harriet close up, in a hat that covered one eye and left the other beckoning.

Finally there were the "Me" pages. "Me, with Harriet at Saratoga." "Me, in the new apt on 85th St." "Me, in my office, 1925." Like the other women in the pictures, "Me" stared back at me suggestively from the sepia prints. Or was it just my imagination? Had I been browsing too long in a shop that time forgot?

The shopkeeper was studying me when I at last looked up. "That's a lovely book, isn't it?" she said. Her ability to know my thoughts was unnerving. I stammered, "Is—is it for sale?" I turned it over and over in my hands, searching for the price.

She took a deep, loud breath through her nose, and the sound filled the room. "I wouldn't know what to charge," she answered. "It belonged to my aunt, Lucy Warner Weir. I leave it out simply to add to the shop's ambience."

"I'd pay whatever you want," I said. Then regretting my desperate tone, I lied quickly, "I collect old photographs."

"What do you do with them?" She continued, as we spoke, to work on her jewelry display.

"Nothing," I said. "Nothing. I just look at them."

"Oh, in that case," she said, giving a final smoothing to the red velvet. I waited expectantly for her next words, hoping they would put the book in my price range. "Perhaps twenty dollars?" "You may have it for twenty-five." But her mouth was set in a firm line and she did not speak.

"Will you take thirty dollars for it?" I ventured, starting at what I thought was high so as not to insult her.

"I have to think about it," she said. "Perhaps you could come back another time. Say, next week. I won't sell it to anyone else before that."

I opened the cover again, my eyes falling on the coy smile and haunting eyes of "Me."

"Please. I'd really like to buy this. Maybe thirty-five? I'd take good care of it."

She glanced past me out the window. "It's stopped raining," she noted. Behind the damask curtain a telephone rang faintly, an old-fashioned tinkle and not the harsh, electronic ring of AT&T. "Excuse me one minute," and she disappeared into the back room.

Then I did something I had never done before and will never do again. Something that haunted me for months. I placed a hastily scrawled check for thirty-five dollars on the glass countertop, with "Pay To The Order Of" left blank, because I hadn't noticed the name of the store. Then I hurried out with the scrapbook tucked into my bag. The doorbell ruined my escape, but I did not turn around to see the shopkeeper's face. I jumped into the nearest cab and directed the driver to my apartment. The bizarre thing is that the check was never cashed.

For weeks, I screened my calls with the answering machine, afraid that the shopkeeper would call and demand the return of the scrapbook. It had been stupid to leave a check with my name at the top, which she could easily use to find me. But I only had a little cash and was not willing to resort to outright theft, and I didn't realize till I was in the cab heading uptown that the check had been a foolish move. Thieves don't leave their calling cards. I can't explain what overtook me in the shop, what feeling of panic and terror that I would never see the faces in the photos again, that when I returned for the book, the shopkeeper would have broken her promise and sold it to the highest bidder. I felt like a criminal, even though I'd left a check and an easy way to trace me. I hid the album under my bed and did not even tell Catherine about it. In fact, I couldn't look at it myself for several weeks. When the notice from the post office arrived, I was convinced I would go to jail.

That Saturday, I came home from staying overnight at Catherine's and found a yellow delivery slip in my mailbox. It wasn't unusual, because I belonged to several book clubs and was always getting packages. I tossed it aside with the rest of my mail and made lunch. Later, I picked up the slip when I was sorting through the bills and fundraising letters. In the space for the description of the article to be claimed, the mail carrier had checked "Certified Letter," and not "Parcel," as usual. At first, I was sure he had made a mistake. Who would be sending me a certified letter? The zipcode of origin read "10199," a strange, phantom number not recognizable like others in Manhattan. I pulled out the phone book and searched through the opening pages till I came to the zipcode map. "10199" did not even seem to exist. My finger traced the contours of Manhattan, up and down, then crosstown. Then I noticed a chart to one side of the map, listing post offices and their corresponding zipcodes. The first on the list was 10199, the James B. Farley Post Office at 421 Eighth Avenue.

A note at the bottom of the page explained how to calculate cross streets by the avenue address. I did it incorrectly once before I came up with Thirty-first Street.

"Thirty-first Street," I said to myself.

I couldn't think of any reason for someone in Manhattan to send me a certified letter. And I didn't know anyone who lived or worked in the vicinity of Thirty-first and Eighth, who might have posted it in that neighborhood. My guilty conscience decided on the answer: It was a notice from the shopkeeper's lawyer, whose office must be in that neighborhood. But I had to wait till Monday morning to find out for sure.

I called Catherine to confirm our dinner plans. "By the way," I said casually, "why do you suppose someone would send me a certified letter?"

"Can't you just open it and find out?" she asked, always practical. She also knew me too well. It would have been like me to sit and stare at a threatening letter instead of opening it.

"I just have the notice that they tried to deliver it," I explained. "It's from the James B. Farley Post Office on Eighth Avenue at Thirty-first Street."

"Hmm," she said. "That usually means something very good or something very bad." She took a drink and the ice cubes rattled in my ear. "Have you been playing Lotto again, or did you enter the Publishers Clearinghouse?"

"I did enter the sweepstakes," I admitted, and I had the useless magazine subscription to U.S. Health to prove it. "But I asked them to send me a telegram if I won." I turned the yellow slip over and read the fine print on the back, which held no further clues. "I'm afraid I'm in big trouble."

"Have you done anything wrong?" Her words echoed in my ears so I thought she said them twice.

"Not that I can think of," I said. "Not that I can think of."

"Well, then," she said, sensibly, ready to move on to another topic, "I guess there's nothing to be worried about."

"Suppose," I continued, and thought I heard her sigh on the other end, "suppose someone's suing me. I mean, this could be something like that, right?"

"Why would anyone sue you?"

My mind raced back to another time I had felt guilty. "That story I published a few years ago. Remember? I used the real name of Fellini's Restaurant and had one of my characters say the food was terrible."

"Oh, Susan," she said, and didn't say anything else.

"Well, I can't find out till Monday." I folded the slip twice into a neat square that didn't show the words "Certified Letter."

"It's probably something stupid," she said. "Something totally inconsequential that didn't really require a certified letter. Someone just did it trying to be important. Now let's forget about it, okay? What time should I meet you?"

I must have said a time, because she responded with "See you then," and hung up.

But I had to call her back a little later to find out what time I had actually said.

♦

Catherine Synge lived on the Lower East Side on Henry Street, a world away from my apartment on the Upper West Side. You could connect our apartments on a map with a sharp diagonal line, but the actual traveling time between the two was formidable. It had almost been the ruin of our relationship several times in the three years we had been together. I was often asking her to move in with me, and she would counter by proposing I move in with her. She liked being downtown, near her job and in the area where she grew up. I liked being uptown, near my classes at Columbia. There seemed to be no good compromise, unless we wanted to meet in the middle, somewhere, I thought, around the Public Library.

We had chosen to eat at Catherine's favorite Chinese restaurant in her neighborhood, on East Broadway. Before I met Catherine, who made it a point to get to know other cultures, I never ventured to the Chinese restaurants deep in Chinatown, but always stayed on the fringes with the other white people. Catherine began taking me to restaurants where we sat at large round tables with Chinese couples, and I learned to eat from my rice bowl and to wield my chopsticks almost as well as she.

At dinner I was drinking Tsing-Tao and beginning to feel a little drunk, like I was going to start to divulge my secret any minute. Catherine was talking earnestly about a women's history conference she was helping to organize. Though I was interested, I couldn't help thinking how she would love the photographs I found, since she was a historian and had mounted several historical photo exhibits in her area of expertise, which was immigration. She asked me a question and I was about to answer with a non sequitur, when I stopped myself.

"Well?" she said, sitting straighter in her chair and looking less animated than she had the moment before.

"I'm sorry," I said helplessly.

She sighed deeply. "Are you still thinking about that letter?" she asked impatiently. "You haven't heard a word I've said, have you?"

"Yes, I have," I said. "I have."

She leaned back in her chair and touched the waitress as she passed, to ask for the bill.

"I'm sorry," I said again. "I really am interested in the conference, you know that. I'm just preoccupied."

I offered to pay for dinner, and she let me.

♦

That night, in Catherine's loft bed, I tossed and turned and almost pushed her out onto the floor. I woke up with her elbow in my side. "Susan," she said, sleepily, "stop it."

I apologized and we switched sides of the mattress.

My dreams were interconnected and fragmented at the same time. I woke up briefly in between them, just to fall back asleep and into the same general dream theme. They were, of course, all about a certified letter and what it might signify.

In the first segment, the IRS discovered that I had cheated on my taxes for the last three years and hadn't claimed five thousand dollars in income. The notice that I had ten days to pay the delinquent taxes plus the fines came in a certified letter.

In the second, the owner of Fellini's Restaurant caught up with me. The letter said, "We've been looking for you for three years. The jig is up." The owner looked a lot like the head of the English Department at school.

In the third, the shopkeeper had hired a detective to track me down. The detective bore a striking resemblance to my first lover.

In the fourth, my mother notified me by certified mail that she and my father were disinheriting me, "because you've been nothing but an embarrassment as a daughter. We heard about your recent arrest for theft. Signed, Your Mother."

In the last, or the last that I remembered, I got a yellowed photograph of "Me and Harriet" in the mail. Their faces peeked out of the envelope coyly, smiling.

◆

On Monday morning I stood on line at the post office for a half hour. The clerk was unusually slow, and the fact that the line was ten people deep didn't seem to bother him. As I approached the window, he excused himself and took, I assumed, a bathroom break.

"Yes?" he said when he returned, as if it were odd to find people waiting on line at his window. I shoved the yellow slip at him roughly, and he took his time finding the envelope.

In the last seconds before he returned to the window, I thought I was going to be sick. I was sure I was going to have to leave the line and find a bathroom or at least some alley where I could throw up. But then he came back, envelope in hand. I tried to read the address through the window, but my eyesight is even worse upside down than it is rightside up.

"Identification," he demanded. "Please sign here," he finished, after comparing my driver's license photo with my face.

Finally, he handed the envelope through the window. This, I thought as I grabbed it, could change the rest of my life.

I was right, in a sense. Because my landlord had raised my rent by ten percent.

◆ 3 ◆

It took about four weeks for me to decide that the shopkeeper was not after me. It was a hard decision to come to, but after I had made it I realized that I no longer remembered exactly what day I had been there or where the shop was. It was as if the scrapbook had come to me in a dream, that I had invented it, and then it appeared under my bed. In fact, I very nearly said to myself, "Oh, look what I found!" when I finally pulled the book from its hiding place.

The thrill of looking through it the second time was even greater than the first, and the third time was even better than both put together. It was on the third pass that I found the courage to lift the photos carefully out of their mounting corners and flip them over.

"Me" had written what she hadn't had room for on the front: the names of the women and the dates the pictures were taken.

It was on the fourth trip through the scrapbook that I was finally able to read those names.

Elinor Devere.

Harriet Timberlake.

Sarah Stern.

Lucy Weir.

1918.

1920.

1926.

1927. And nothing later.

By the fifth pass I was in love with each and every one of

them. I memorized their individual smiles. I could mimic the way Harriet raised her left eyebrow slightly in a flirtation with the camera. I had picked out Elinor's nervous habit of rubbing the cuticle of her thumb with her index finger. I recognized Sarah as an ardent feminist. I had determined that Lucy had been in love with Harriet for a long time.

On the sixth perusal, I became convinced that I had been the photographer.

"Smile, ladies," I said. "Say pretty please."

"Pretty pu-lease," said Harriet.

"Pretty please hurry," said Elinor.

"Please," said Sarah, "can't you ever remember that women are more than just pretty?"

"Harriet," said Lucy.

During the seventh pass, I realized the obvious: that Elinor and Sarah were a couple. It seemed to me that I had known this fact all along but had simply forgotten it while taking the pictures. I had been so caught up in the moment, I had actually asked Elinor to have dinner with me.

"And Sarah, too?" she had asked.

"Why, of course," I replied, embarrassed at my lapse of memory.

Then Elinor leaned over and kissed Sarah on the cheek, and something in the way she did it made me think of Catherine.

Harriet slipped her arm through mine, making it difficult to manage the camera. Hesitantly, I took the shot without her in it.

"And what is the name of that delightful partner of yours?" she asked, squeezing my arm ever so slightly. "The beautiful history teacher?"

"Catherine," I answered, advancing the film. "Catherine Synge."

"Catherine Synge," she repeated, melodically. "Catherine Synge. Harriet Timberlake."

I turned and caught on film the moment when she said her own name.

Lucy took my other arm. "Now me," she demanded, and I

obliged. She pulled off her hat and shook her auburn hair. "Capture me for history."

The camera turned into the scrapbook in my hands. I felt the smooth leather cautiously, aware that it contained the future as well as the past.

♦

I began to go to them in daydreams. I went to them with questions on my lips.

What was it like for you then?

Where was your work? What did you eat? What books did you cry over? What was a kiss like in 1926? How did women find each other?

How did I find you?

"Silly girl," said Harriet, with a smile that melted butter, "we found *you*."

♦

"What's this?" Catherine asked, from the living room. I was chopping vegetables at the kitchen counter, watching her anxiously as she made her way to the coffee table and touched the leather scrapbook with one soft hand. "Susan," she said, unaware that I had waited for this moment for weeks, "what's this?"

"Open it up," I said, trying to be casual but nearly chopping my finger into the eggplant.

I thought she gave a little gasp as she opened it, but it was probably me. She had only turned two or three pages when she said, "Where did you find this?"

"At an antiques store downtown," I answered, giving up the chopping to stand beside her as she lingered over the pages. "It was raining."

She nodded as if to say she understood. "Who are they?"

I recited their names in a litany.

"Oh," she said. Then, "1920. 1926."

"Yes," I said, aware all along that she would know the dates exactly, without having to look at the backs of the photos.

She closed the cover gently. "I can't remember," she said, "when I've heard of something this extraordinary. Finding a lesbian scrapbook in an antiques shop."

I smiled.

"They're just beautiful," Catherine said, opening the cover again.

"Catherine," said Harriet and Lucy in unison. "Catherine Synge."

♦

I kept the scrapbook on the shelf with the other lesbian books I had collected. The vitality of Lucy, Harriet and The Gang seemed to give new life to them. Sometimes, when I was in the bedroom, I heard some unexplained racket in the living room and became convinced that it was The Gang, having a little get-together on the bookshelf.

The women didn't live for Catherine the way they did for me, but I shared the book with her anyway. She was, after all, a historian of women, rational but sensitive all at the same time. But I was hesitant to tell her the experience I was having with The Gang. Catherine had related many stores about growing up in her traditional Irish family, in which her immigrant grandmother talked a lot about spirits and saints and other seemingly fantastic things. She had rebelled against it at a young age; and even though she felt she had a deeper appreciation of her culture now, she still drew the line at all things magical. Partly because of that, she'd gone into history, the discipline that depends on fact.

We spent many evenings those first few weeks at my apartment pouring over the scrapbook. It was now my favorite thing to do. I refused to travel with the book, I was afraid of loose photographs falling out all over Manhattan. I couldn't bear the thought of losing even one mounting corner.

17

Our ritual on those evenings was to bring in dinner and eat it quickly while filling each other in on our days. Then Catherine made a pot of tea, we curled up together on the couch, and I brought the scrapbook from the shelf. It was better than a Katherine Hepburn movie on TV, better than reading books together as we fell asleep in bed.

Catherine noticed everything. She had an eye for detail in photographs. She could describe the texture of their clothes. She could tell how old a picture was by the length of someone's skirt. She could read the fine print on a book Harriet was holding in one of the photographs.

"It looks like *The Intrepid Ones*," Catherine said, her nose just inches from the photo. I was sure that Harriet would say something to complain, but she didn't. "Mean anything to you?"

It was a title I probably would have pulled off a bookshelf to inspect, but I did not remember ever doing so. "It sounds a little like a sixties TV show," I laughed.

Catherine squinted at the photograph in a way that must have been less than attractive from Harriet and Lucy's end. "There's a name, too," she said, and for a moment I thought she was going to climb into the shot, walk up to Harriet, and say, "Excuse me, that sounds like an interesting book. May I ask who the author is?"

"If you have a magnifying glass," Catherine said instead, "I could probably make it out."

I had one that had come with the Oxford English Dictionary I had ordered from one of my book clubs. Catherine moved it up and down over the photo, zooming it back and forth to get a clearer view. I wanted to suggest we just ask Harriet, but Catherine was having fun playing the detective historian. "Well, whaddya know," she said, freezing the magnifying glass in place. Before she said anything, I felt I knew the answer. Because just a second before Catherine told me, Harriet had whispered in my ear.

"Lucy Warner Weir," they both said, a second apart.

◆

It was Catherine's idea to begin researching the women in the scrapbook. She said it would be easy, not like her own work, which had involved trips to Boston and once overseas. I could just go halfway to her house, to the Public Library. I already knew their names and the approximate time they lived. And now I knew that Lucy was an author. I could probably find the book somewhere. Maybe it could form the basis of my dissertation. She said it would be fun.

It all seemed like a lot of work to me, because I was convinced they would tell me their stories eventually and far more accurately than written records could. Catherine had no interest in taking on another research project, because she was deeply involved in her own projects, especially the same work on Irish women's immigration she'd been doing when we met. And I knew she would find it hard to justify doing research on privileged, middle-class women, even if they were lesbians. Catherine's work had all focused on the working class, where her roots were. Her mother had worked all her life as a waitress, and her father drove a cab. "I could help, though," she said. "You could do a whole exhibit around these photos, maybe for Gay Pride Week."

I smiled hesitantly. I was not so sure I wanted to share them. I found it a little comforting that even Catherine couldn't speak to them directly. I was concerned about it, because Harriet was very flirtatious and had described Catherine as beautiful. She was most beautiful now while she was thinking quickly, more quickly than she could get the words out of her mouth. She sat twisting one end of her long red hair, the way she did in her most intense moments, her deep green eyes darting back and forth as if she were watching pictures in her head. A faint smile parted her lips. She was thinking about history, and for a moment time melted away. I wondered if Harriet was whispering her name, and I felt jealous because I couldn't hear anything.

Then she was back. "You could get your dissertation out of this. Yes, I really think you should do it," Catherine said decisively. "You've been entrusted with history, Susan. It's your responsibility."

I sighed. "Maybe," I said, "maybe they wouldn't like being exposed like that."

Catherine laughed a high-pitched giggle unlike her own. I am sure it was really Harriet's. "Oh, come on," she said, holding up a photo of Harriet and Lucy with their arms linked, their playful eyes teasing the camera. "These women are *begging* to be exposed."

I had to agree. Because as she held the photo up, Harriet winked at me.

♦

The next morning, after Catherine had left for her teaching job, I was taking some last bites of toast before I had to be off, too. I stood staring down at the open scrapbook on my coffee table.

"Ladies," I said, "Catherine's right. You've entrusted me with history. I'm the caretaker of your lives. You've got to help me out with this. We're in this together."

There was no answer. Perhaps they were still asleep. In fact, I heard a yawn that was not my own. Through the yawn, I thought I heard someone say, "All right."

◆ 4 ◆

I was in the second year of the doctoral program in English at Columbia. It was, I thought, what I had always wanted. My whole life pointed toward literature and writing, starting at about age seven, when I began to write stories. I had no idea what my dissertation topic would be, and I had no idea what I would do with this degree if I ever finished it. Probably stack the diploma in the closet with the others, the B.A. and teaching certificate from the University of Chicago, the M.F.A. in writing from San Francisco State, the M.B.A. from Fordham. I had crisscrossed the country stacking up degrees I never used, or at least not for more than a few months at a time. In between, I supported myself with substitute teaching assignments, telemarketing jobs, stints as a waitress, and loans from Grandmother Van Dine. I owed her close to twenty thousand dollars by the time I was thirty. I owed the government even more in student loans.

As a teaching assistant, I had to teach one freshman English composition class. Then I spent a lot of time grading papers from an associate professor's American lit survey. It was all very routine and not too interesting. The students were bright enough but smart-mouthed, at the age when they believed that being freshmen at Columbia made them a special breed. Most of them took English because it was required, not out of any love for the language and how it's put together. More often than not, a fifth of the students enrolled in the class didn't show up. Sometimes I thought it was no better than teaching in a public high school, except that I didn't fear for my life. I often thought I would be much happier across the street at Barnard, where at least I might have had some young lesbians in my class, or at City College, where less privileged students were more appreciative of the learning process.

After I found the scrapbook, I began to prepare for class less and less and to give in-class writing assignments more and more. It required little effort on my part, except that I had to listen to the students' groans and sighs. I gave them topics from classes I had had as a student. Then they wrote for thirty minutes, and we spent fifteen minutes hearing people's reactions to the assignment. Then I collected them and read them quickly at lunch, checking for nouns and verbs. I am not sure they were learning anything except how to write under pressure. But I was allowing myself more time to daydream about Lucy and her gang.

It was in the middle of one of my reveries that Lucy said, "If you can't do it anymore, you might as well quit."

The thought had occurred to me, but I hadn't entertained it for too long. What would I do this time? Had I finally had my fill of school? Had it ceased to challenge me? Catherine had been so supportive of this degree. When Catherine and I met, we were both doing volunteer work for a feminist newspaper. She wrote pithy news articles, and I kept the books. I pursued her until she noticed me. But I was finishing up my M.B.A., and Catherine wasn't sure she could, in good conscience, go out with anyone in business school who was, she suspected, trying to get a niche in the male establishment.

But my motivation for going to business school had won her over. "It's just a diversion," I explained. "I wanted to see how the other half thinks. I'll never use it."

And true to my word, I hadn't. You hardly need an M.B.A. to sell credit card theft protection plans by phone.

"I think," Catherine decided, "you should go on for your doctorate. You'll just wander aimlessly till you do."

I had to agree with her. Catherine was brilliant, someone who had made the most out of a minimum of degrees. She had been teaching high school history since graduating from Hunter College, which she had worked her way through. She had started an M.A. in night school, but gave it up because it was too structured and didn't allow enough time for the research projects she wanted to do. Most of her advanced knowledge was picked up casually, through voracious reading. She had also spent a lot of time talking to older people on the Lower East Side, rummaging through their photos, recording their lives, and putting them into exhibits.

But she knew me very well. She knew I did not have that kind of self-direction. I belonged in graduate school; I was the sort of person for whom it was invented. I needed a dissertation hanging over my head to get me to work. Without it I would spend my days serving lunches to business executives, my nights pasted in front of the TV with the remote control firmly in my hand.

I trusted Catherine's knowledge of me. I trusted her recommendations. I valued her opinion and feared her disapproval. She was, after all, a minor genius, who had chosen me as her lover and hadn't left me yet. So it was with a great deal of difficulty that I walked into the office of the chair of the English Department and announced that I needed a leave of absence, starting immediately. Seven months, I said, just summer term and fall semester. Why? I couldn't say I'm bored, I'm distracted, so I told the only other truth there was. "For a research project," I said. "It will take all my time for seven months."

But something told me I had no intention of going back. I emptied my desk in the cubbyhole I shared with another T.A. and went home to lie on my bed and think up something to tell Catherine.

♦

The same day I quit Columbia, I got a package in the mail. It was painstakingly wrapped in layer after layer of heavy brown paper, sealed with waterproof tape, the frustrating kind you try to tear first and then have to cut through to remove. There was no return address. The package was addressed to me with my middle name, which I used only for official papers and my financial records: Susan Abigail Van Dine.

Inside was a 1922 first edition of *The Intrepid Ones*. It was in excellent condition, except for some wear at the corners of the cover where it had been repeatedly taken on and off the shelf. Inside was scrawled in faded blue ink, "For H., my partner and friend."

Someone had placed a sheet of linen stationery inside. It took a minute for me to realize the note was new, not something from the twenties. It, too, had been written with an old fountain pen.

"For your collection," it said. There was no name, but I knew immediately that it was from the shopkeeper. I don't think Lucy told me. I think I knew simply from the fluttery feeling in my stomach when the dusty smell of the antiques shop wafted up from the folds of the wrapping.

♦

I decided that the best way to avoid Catherine's disapproval was not to tell her about my leave of absence. I rarely spoke to her during the day, because when she was not in class she was preparing lesson plans or advising the student History Club or off at the Public Library doing her own research. If at night she asked about my day, I could launch into some story of student unrest. I had a good, on-the-spot imagination. I realized she might never have to know I had left at all. And if I were gathering information about Lucy and The Gang, that would satisfy her that I was definitely as busy and hard at work as she was.

Catherine was getting tired of always coming to my apartment. The novelty of the scrapbook had worn off for her, and she didn't understand why I wanted to look at it every night.

"You haven't been to my place in weeks," she complained on the phone. "Why do I always have to do the traveling?"

"I have something to show you," I said, avoiding her complaint. "I can't wait for you to see it."

"Bring it here," she said, wearily. "We'll have dinner out, and you can tell me all about it."

"I'm afraid something will happen to it."

"Take a cab." She sighed heavily into the phone. "My treat."

"But it goes with the scrapbook," I insisted. "We need to look at them both to get the full effect."

There was a long, important silence from Catherine's end. "I can't tonight," she said finally. "I'm too beat. Maybe tomorrow."

I don't remember begging her to come or calling her Harriet, but she says that I did. And Catherine is almost always right.

♦

In the end, I was relieved that Catherine had stayed home. I was up all night reading *The Intrepid Ones*. In the morning I went right on reading, as if time had no meaning and the only thing that mattered was finishing the novel. When I finally looked up from the last page, it was evening again and Catherine was calling to say she wouldn't be over that night either.

"Are you seeing someone else?" I asked, knowing that she wasn't.

"Don't be ridiculous," she said. "Are you?"

"No," I said, with a sudden warm blush of guilt. Because just as I finished reading, just as the phone was ringing, I had been masturbating with *The Intrepid Ones* beside me on the bed.

"I got a copy of *The Intrepid Ones*," I blurted out. "I think I got the actual copy Harriet's holding in the picture."

"You're kidding," she said. "How did you do that?"

"I went back to the shop where I bought the scrapbook," I lied. I thought Catherine, who had high moral standards, would have left me in a second if she ever found out how I really got the scrapbook. "It was just a hunch. She had a copy— I couldn't believe it. It's inscribed 'For H., my partner and friend.'"

"That could be anyone," the historian warned me. "Don't

jump to conclusions. Does it match the writing in the scrap-book?"

"That was printed, this is in script. But it seems coincidental to me," I said. "Doesn't it seem coincidental to you?"

"You'll need to find some letters or something to confirm it," Catherine said, and I imagined her twisting her hair in thought at the other end. "A writer must have left letters. You just need to determine where she would have left them."

I was deep in silent protestation. I *knew* Lucy had written it. I knew without doing research. I opened the cover and ran my index finger over the faded ink of the inscription. "Trust yourself," I heard someone say, and it wasn't Catherine.

◆

The Intrepid Ones was the story of a group of career women in New York City in the early 1900s. It was not specifically lesbian, but two of the women lived together in what was known then as a "Boston marriage." The characters were strong, but the writing was old-fashioned, peppered with dashes and semicolons and flowery sentences that seemed to go on for pages. I loved it. It had the flavor of old New York. I read it two times in the first week. I began to hear the clip-clop of horses out my window, the clack of streetcars, the tinkle of the bell and the treble of the conductor's call. I fully expected to get up at some point and look out the window and discover I was living in 1910.

I didn't see Catherine at all that week. She said she was busy with the history conference, but I wasn't so sure. She asked about classes and I said they were the same. I said I had been spending some time at the library, reading old newspapers and looking for a review of *The Intrepid Ones*. She seemed to believe it, but probably wondered why she hadn't run into me. If she thought I was lying, she didn't say.

That week away from Catherine, I started doing a funny thing. Something I'm embarrassed to admit. But I've admitted the stolen scrapbook, so what could be worse? At nights, I

started propping a picture of Lucy and Harriet on the nightstand beside my bed. I tried putting a picture of the whole
Gang there, but that was too discomforting, like a crowd of
people was watching me sleep. So I substituted the picture of
Lucy and Harriet. While Lucy watched, Harriet sang me to
sleep with "I'll See You in My Dreams." She had a lovely
voice.

"I'm an actress, my dear," she told me when I complimented her. "My voice is my living."

Lucy whistled softly as Harriet sang. I fell asleep soundly,
deeply, pleasantly, with the sensation that someone was fond-
ling my breasts.

♦

Friday evening Catherine surprised me at the door with a
carton of mu shu vegetables and another of curry chicken.

"My favorites," I smiled.

"I missed you," she said, folding her arms and the cartons
around me. "Why am I always the one who has to make up?"

I couldn't answer, because she was kissing me hard, deep,
with an insistence that made my knees buckle. When she released me, she said decisively, "I think we should live together. After all, your rent's going up. It's the perfect time."

"For you to move in here?" I asked hopefully.

"God, no. I'd be stupid to move out of a rent-controlled
apartment," she said, laying out the food on the coffee table
with rice bowls and chopsticks. "If you moved in with me, it
would be so cheap. One-forty-five a month for each of us."
She must have expected the hesitant look on my face. I was
still standing at the door. She left the food and came toward
me in a hot rush. Her mouth was on mine again, her tongue
darting in and out with silky speed.

She had my pants unbuttoned before I knew what was
happening. She pushed them down to my knees adeptly with
one hand and gripped my waist with the other. In one quick,
sure movement she was inside me, with two, three fingers,

maybe more. I groaned with the sudden sweet memory of what sex with Catherine was like. I had almost forgotten, in one short week.

She pushed into me harder as she knelt down and took me with her tongue, the hard, confident tongue I knew so well. It didn't take long. As I came, I grabbed her head and pushed it firmly against me. She was still holding my waist so I wouldn't fall over. There was a sweet, sharp pain between my legs as her fingers slipped out. She wiped her mouth delicately on my bush, as she would later on her napkin, after we ate.

"That'll give you something to think about," she said, rebuttoning my pants. Then she served dinner. It was still piping hot.

♦

I woke up in the middle of the night with the same sensation as before, of someone touching my breasts. Catherine was sound asleep on her side, facing the wall. The picture of Lucy and Harriet, which I had hurriedly flipped over so Catherine wouldn't see it, was standing upright on the nightstand. They were watching us, with the faintly amused and intrigued smiles of voyeurs.

Then in my dreams I thought I saw Lucy and Harriet having sex. Two figures were tucked away under an enormous quilt in a massive rosewood sleigh bed that dwarfed both of them. Every now and then I spied a bare arm or leg or buttock and heard a satisfied moan. In the morning, the picture of them was face down again, exactly the way I had left it.

◆ 5 ◆

I calculated how far my savings would take me. Then I took a part-time job at an antiques and junk shop called Out of Time, on upper Broadway not far from my apartment.

The shop bore no resemblance to the one where I had found the scrapbook. There was more junk than antiques. Baskets and barrels heaped with old clutter lined the floor. The furniture was stacked one piece on top of another. The books filled empty liquor store boxes. There was a table of broken stuff outside with a hastily scrawled sign that said, "Your pick—25¢."

The shop was owned by a woman who I thought may have been a lesbian. She didn't look like one, but she looked at women as if she were. She wore huge, brightly colored caftans with strands of love beads around her neck. Time had stopped for her somewhere around 1968. Her name was Marjorie, but everyone called her Margielove. She had a streak of bright blond running across the right side of her long black hair, and she touched my arm lightly with fingers covered in costume jewelry rings.

She had hired me on the spot. I saw the sign in the window for part-time help and I wandered in, pretending to shop for mismatched silver. I took to the register two F.B. Rogers soup spoons and a knife.

"It's four for a dollar," she said, and I went back and fished another spoon out of the silverware basket.

"You must eat a lot of soup," she chuckled, eyeing me in a cool, possessive way.

"I collect spoons," I lied then added quickly, "and an occasional knife."

"One-oh-eight," she said, her bedecked fingers drumming the glass of the counter. She put the silver into a crinkled, ratty-looking paper bag that said Duane Reade Drugs on the front.

I paid and stood thumbing through a shoebox of postcards on the counter. I picked out one, a hand-tinted photo of a bunch of roses, and another, a view of the Public Library in 1926.

"And these," I said.

"You collect postcards, too," she snickered. "And what else?"

"That's all today," I said.

"No, I mean what else do you collect?" she persisted.

I hesitated and watched her fingers tapping the countertop. I wanted to reach over and stop them, but gently.

"Photographs from the 1920s," I said. "And books." I watched her eyes watch me. There was kindness somewhere behind them. "Lesbian books," I ventured.

"Well," she said, sucking in a deep breath, "we don't get too many of those. Of course, no one's ever straightened out the mess here to see what we really have. I just bought this joint six months ago. I'd like to clean it up some."

I put down another $2.16 for the postcards, thinking it was an unusual pricing system that valued paper higher than sterling silver.

"I need a job," I said suddenly, surprising myself more than her.

"Can you start tomorrow?" she asked. As it turned out, I could. I had nothing else to do, but sit and wait to hear from Lucy.

◆

It was an ideal job for me at that time. I got to wear jeans and t-shirts and rummage through someone else's mess. Margielove let me start with the books. Besides the boxes in the store, a quarter of the cellar was stacked with decaying books.

Since I was only getting six dollars an hour, Margielove cut me a deal. "Anything you find that you want, take it," she said, adding, "within reason." The most appealing thing about Margielove was she trusted me without knowing me. Something in my face, she said. She would have been surprised to hear about my theft of the scrapbook. Or maybe not. She was the kind of woman who looked like she had seen everything at least once, and maybe two or three times.

There were old bookshelves in the basement covered with dusty, broken curios. Over the first few weeks, I emptied the junk into boxes, then cleaned and refinished the shelves. Margielove paid two neighborhood boys to carry them from the basement to the shop, where it was hard to tell if they added anything or not.

"It's a start," she said.

Then I went to work on the books in the shop. A lot of them were worthless from mildew. We placed them on the twenty-five cents table outside. Most of the others were second and third printings of old novels I had never heard of that people would probably never buy. We kept them inside and charged fifty cents apiece for them.

"At least they look good," Margielove said.

The books in the basement were mostly a disappointment. They were severely water-damaged from a thin leak from some unknown source. We ended up putting most of them on the sidewalk for the street people. They disappeared one by one, which pleased Margielove.

"It's a service to the community," she observed.

After two weeks, when I had given up discovering anything I wanted, I made an incredible find. The binding was completely ripped off, but I could still read the title page, *An Economic History of American Women* by Sarah Stern, published in 1920. I had almost forgotten her. She had barely looked at me from the scrapbook, she had hardly said a word. The inscription was smudged and dirty, but indelible. It read, "For my partners in crime, Love, Sarah." Stuck between two pages in the middle of the book was a yellowed newspaper clipping from a Saratoga Springs newspaper. Someone had marked at the top in blue ink, "June 24, 1919. Harriet a star. Yippee!" The clipping was a review of a play called *Miss Morley*. Part of it was circled with the same blue pen.

Miss Harriet Timberlake of 223 W. 85 St. in New York City made a stunning debut last night in the title role of Christina Morley. Her flawless delivery stands her with the great comic actresses of our time. It is a credit to her talent that she gave a memorable performance in an otherwise less than memorable play. This reviewer hopes to see more of her soon, in a vehicle that would match her considerable gifts.

Now I had proof for Catherine. The writing on the clipping matched the inscription in Lucy's book.

♦

I began to suspect that Catherine was suspicious. I had even gone to her apartment one evening to allay apprehensions. She seemed to be asking "How's summer term?" or "Is the campus pretty quiet?" more often than she should have. And I was running out of things to say and stories to tell. I had started recalling incidents from my college days as if they had happened yesterday in class. When Catherine came over, I would pretend I had work of my own to do and would excuse myself for an hour to do it. She wasn't very curious about it— she had found, in the past, my discussions of minute points of American literary criticism extremely dull.

But she did want to know about Lucy.

"And how's your favorite research topic coming along?" she asked.

"Well," I said, "you're not going to believe this, but I found a book by Sarah Stern."

Of course, she asked, "Where?"

I thought quickly and decided the antiques shop where I

got the scrapbook was the best bet. I could milk it for a while, as long as Catherine didn't want to know exactly where it was.

"At the shop again, the antiques shop. I gave the shop-keeper my number, so she's on the lookout for stuff. This is the most amazing find." I ran into the bedroom to get it for her. From their place on the nightstand Lucy and Harriet looked out at me blankly, with no emotion or sign of life. I flipped them onto their faces.

Catherine read the clipping with great interest. Then she held it next to the inscription in *The Intrepid Ones*. "Yep, it's the same hand," she said. "I guess you're assuming it's Lucy's."

I *know* it's Lucy's, I wanted to scream. I was tiring of the conscientious historian who would never believe anything without a small library of corroborating material. "Yes," I said.

"It still doesn't have her name anywhere," Catherine said doubtfully. "It's probably a safe assumption, but you need to find some letters, a diary. Any luck so far?" She was twisting her hair with ideas.

"No," I said.

"So when did she die?" Catherine asked suddenly. "What were her dates?"

I looked at her quizzically, as if she had just turned into Dr. Hammill, my college history professor, right before my eyes. In fact, I thought I heard her voice lower a pitch and saw some black hairs sprout on her upper lip. I turned away quickly, afraid that when I glanced back she would be smoking a pipe.

"I don't know," I admitted, foolishly I realized. "Does it matter?" It was hard for me to think of Lucy as having "dates," someone who was and then was no more. Under the circumstances, it seemed preposterous.

"Does it matter!" she repeated. "Oh, now I see what the problem is! I encourage you to do historical research, but you don't have the slightest idea how to go about it!" She smiled at my historical innocence. "I'll tell you what. The conference is this weekend, and after it's over I'll have more time. Why don't I call the Lesbian Archives and make an appointment for us? They *must* have something about these women, Lucy and Sarah at the very least."

I nodded weakly. I couldn't think quickly enough to protest.

♦

I still had a few weeks to decide about renewing the lease. The apartment had been a burden all along, but now at ten percent more, with me earning only a hundred and fifty a week and getting no assistantship money, it was an enormous load.

On a whim, I walked down to Eighty-fifth Street and found Number 223, a turn-of-the-century building with seven floors. To my amazement, I rang the bell for the super.

"Yeah?" came a scratchy woman's voice over the intercom.

"Any vacancies?" I asked.

"Well," she said, not at all sure she should talk to me, "I'll be right out."

She took a look at me through the door and decided I was all right to talk to. She patted her housedress into place. "You need an apartment?"

"Yes," I lied. "My building's gone co-op."

"Well, I shouldn't tell you this, but a lady died not too long ago. A real nice apartment. The boss has been wanting her out for a long time. Rent control, y'know. But it looks like the woman who took care of her might stay on. Her name's on the lease, too, it turns out. But we'll have to wait and see what she plans to do." She pulled back a minute, afraid she had said too much. Real estate in New York can be a vicious business. "If she leaves, I'm sure it'll go up to five or six times higher, maybe more. They'll renovate it." She took in my blue jeans and denim jacket and must have concluded I was only imitation yuppie. "You don't look like you could afford it," she finished, starting to close the door on me.

"Wait," I said. "At least give me the landlord's number, so I can keep in touch." She glared at me, her eyes filming over like sheets of dirty glass. I dug in my pocket and pulled out ten dollars, a good portion of my pay for the week.

She rattled off the number, and for want of a better place to put it, I wrote it on my arm. When I tried to dial it later, it had been temporarily disconnected.

◆

That was the beginning of a short dry period. I felt like Lucy and Harriet had left me. In the photographs, they looked like cardboard figures. The life and sparkle had gone out of their eyes. Or maybe it had gone from me. I didn't know who I was anymore, or what I was doing. At thirty-two years old I had a lot of worthless sheepskins in the closet and no prospects for the future. I would be lucky to make my next rent payment. I was lying nonstop to everyone, including my lover. I had become one big living deception. Worst of all was the temporary loss of my friends from another time.

"Do you believe in time travel?" I asked Margielove one day as I was sprawled out in the shop, organizing the postcards into neat categories. "How about voices from the past?"

She looked at me cautiously from behind pink, heart-shaped sunglasses. I thought her the perfect person to ask, because she was frozen in the sixties.

She was, I'm sure, about to say "Yes." She was about to tell me all the voices she had heard, Jimi Hendrix and Janis and Malcolm X. But just as she was opening her mouth, just as the words were forming, I picked out of the shoebox an old postcard from Montauk and flipped it over. In a familiar hand, I read, "Dearest S., Had to get away from the city. The weather's beautiful, the beach a dream. Hope you're getting on without us. Kisses, L. and H."

I must have gasped or cried out, because Margielove was suddenly beside me, towering over me in her fluorescent pink caftan. "What is it?" she said. "You turned completely white." I handed her the postcard, which she read without surprise. "Someone you know?" she asked.

When I looked at it again, I realized I was going crazy.

The handwriting was totally foreign, the card addressed to "Miss Gertrude Blair" in Hicksville, N.Y. "Dear Friend," it said, "Did you have a good time last night? Best wishes, N.S." I stared up at Margielove in disbelief.

"Kind of funny," she said, reading it once again.

"I have to go home now," I said, and she agreed without asking questions.

As I was barreling out of the door, with Margielove saying, "Take care, Susan," from behind me, I plowed right into Catherine, who was on her way to my apartment. It was our night to go to the Lesbian Archives.

"Susan," she said, taking me by both arms. I was shaking under her touch. "You look like you've seen a ghost. What is it?"

"Catherine," I said softly, feeling like I was melting into the sidewalk, "take me home."

♦

Later, after I'd taken a nap, I stood staring at Catherine in a confused way from the doorway of the bedroom. I felt a little like an amnesia victim who is just regaining memory.

"What happened back there?" she asked. I remained in the doorway, bracing myself on the door frame with both hands.

"I was hallucinating," I said.

"About what? And what were you doing in that shop? Don't you have to teach class today?"

I sat down next to her on the couch, and she offered me the box of saltines she'd been nibbling from. I took one and bit it in half.

"Things are becoming too real," I said.

"What things?" she persisted, but I didn't answer. Instead I picked up the scrapbook from its place on the coffee table. "Susan," Catherine said, sternly, "do we have to do that now?"

I flipped through to the photos of The Gang at Montauk. They stood in a tight line, their arms entwined, perched on a precipice overlooking the sea at Montauk Point. If they had been fragile women, they would have blown away.

But they stood their ground, a firm and impenetrable chain. Elinor, the tallest and sturdiest, held onto her hat. Sarah, beside her, let her hair blow wildly across her face. Harriet, next, pushed her hair aside so everyone could see her clearly. Lucy, at the other end, the second tallest, looked longingly sideways at Harriet.

Did I really, I wondered, take the picture?

"I'm sorry," I said to Catherine, "what did you say?"

"I said, were you hallucinating about these women? Susan, can you hear me?" Her voice was getting louder and louder, as if she believed hallucinations could destroy your hearing. Or maybe because she could see I was somewhere else.

And then, as if by the power of suggestion, I was. I was lowering the camera to my side.

"Thank you," I smiled, "for the lovely postcard. I was worried about you."

"Everyone needs some time away," Harriet said.

"We should be getting back soon," Elinor pointed out, smoothing her skirt and stepping away from the cliff. "Sarah has a meeting to attend."

"You shouldn't worry," Lucy said, maybe to me, maybe to Elinor.

"I'm worried about you," someone was saying, and I could tell by the long, cool fingers pressing into my arm that it was Catherine.

"You shouldn't worry." I smiled. I looked down at my watch. "We have an appointment, don't we? At the Archives?"

"Oh, shit," she said. "I totally forgot to cancel."

I closed the scrapbook and replaced it on the table. "So let's keep it," I said.

◆ 6 ◆

I had been to the Archives once two years before with Catherine, on a volunteer night. She had been working with them for some time, helping them to catalog their voluminous periodical collection. It was work I was not cut out for. I had gotten bored, started checking off periodicals on the list by mistake, and, after a while, excused myself to scan the old novels on the bookshelves. That was where I had picked up the names of authors like Vin Packer. Catherine was embarrassed by my behavior and from then on went alone to volunteer nights.

Roz greeted us warmly at the door. She and Catherine talked for a while about the success of the women's history conference and about Catherine's work on immigration. Then Catherine spoke for me.

"Susan made a wonderful find," she said, poking me so I would hear my cue. I had refused to bring the entire album, but I had wrapped some of the best photos and carried them in my bag. "A photo album from the twenties."

Roz was probably expecting to see the entire album and looked at me curiously when I drew out a small package instead.

"She doesn't like to travel with it," Catherine explained, and because that sounded pathetic, even to me, I found my voice.

"It's fragile," I explained, "and falling apart."

"Oh, of course," Roz said, kindly.

We spread the pictures out on a long table and stood in a row, examining them. Roz turned them over carefully but casually, just like Catherine did, just like a person familiar with history.

"Do you know any of them?" Catherine asked. "I thought maybe, by chance, they were members of Heterodoxy or one of the other women's clubs."

Heterodoxy, I knew from Catherine, had been a New York City feminist society that held regular luncheon meetings in the early to mid-1900s.

"Sarah Stern, definitely," she said, enthusiastically. "And Lucy Weir for a short time. The others, no. Harriet was Lucy's lover, I recognize the name."

"And Elinor, Sarah's," I put in, forgetting I had no basis for that knowledge, except that I had heard it from Elinor's own mouth.

Catherine broke in, "Well, probably, but we don't know for sure."

"Unfortunately, I don't really know anything about their private lives," Roz said, staring at the Montauk shot. "Sarah was an economic historian and labor organizer. She wrote a couple of books that never had much impact because of her radical politics and the fact that she didn't have any degrees. She was, I think, good friends with Crystal Eastman and others, like Elizabeth Gurley Flynn. I knew she never married, but no one's confirmed she was a lesbian. I have a file on her here, some articles she wrote before 1920, if you'd like to see them."

"That would be great. And Lucy?" Catherine asked, smiling sideways at me.

"Lucy was a novelist and English teacher. She taught at Barnard for years. Her writing was too woman-identified, it never quite caught on, like, say, Helen Hull's, which was straighter. I believe she and Harriet were together for quite a while."

"Harriet was an actress," Catherine said. "Ring any bells?"

Roz picked up a photo of Harriet and looked at it thoughtfully, as if willing the photo to tell her. But Harriet, the minx, spoke only to me.

"No, sorry," she said, shaking her head.

"And what about Elinor?" Catherine asked. "We haven't a clue on her."

"Sarah's papers are at NYU and Vassar, if I remember correctly. But it's all public, not her private correspondence. Nothing about Elinor."

"And Lucy's papers?" Catherine pursued. "Do you know where they are?"

"Privately held," she replied, shaking her head, "by a niece who won't release them. Too embarrassing, she says. She may have even destroyed them by now. She lives upstate, in Glens Falls, and she's a little forgetful and pretty unpleasant. Her name's Letty King. I can give you her number."

Before we left, Roz xeroxed Sarah's file for us and pulled out some others on Heterodoxy. She had, in random notes, about as much information as she had already given us about Sarah and Lucy.

"Oh, look, their dates!" Catherine exclaimed, scribbling furiously onto the sheet Roz had given us. "Lucy Warner Weir, 1890-?, born Glens Falls, NY. Sarah Stern, 1890-1964, born New York City. This will be a big help."

I felt superfluous, detached, as if Catherine and Roz could have carried on for hours without me. I was, it seemed, mostly the carrier of the pictures, but then I knew I was closer to all of them than these two historians would ever be. I tucked them carefully away in my knapsack after we finished and pulled several dollars out of my wallet to stuff into their contribution jar.

"Good luck," Roz said, more to Catherine than to me, I thought. "Nice to meet you," she smiled in my direction.

"Well, there's a real start for you," Catherine said, on the way down in the elevator. "I knew this was the best way to begin. Don't you feel a lot better now?"

I nodded, only because I was relieved to see a question mark behind Lucy's name in place of a death date.

♦

When we got home, Catherine was still in her detective mode. "Don't you want to call Letty King?" she asked, while I laid out the Cuban sandwiches we brought in for dinner. "Set up an appointment to try to see Lucy's papers?"

"It's almost nine," I said. "I'll call tomorrow."

"How many people do you know who go to bed at nine?" she laughed, pulling out the paper with the number on it. "Come on, aren't you dying to find out about Lucy?"

In fact, I was, but I liked my own methods. I liked taking their pictures, having them share themselves with me little by little. I wanted this to last, to have a real relationship with all of them. I didn't like having them become public property. These were *my* women; *I* found them. How could I explain this to Catherine?

So I ignored her. She sighed with exasperation and dialed the number. I went into the bedroom with my sandwich and turned on the radio. I sat on the bed and leafed through the Sarah Stern file. The second-generation xeroxes were hard to read.

Minutes later, Catherine stood in the doorway with her sandwich. "May I?" she asked, nodding toward the bed.

"Please," I said, setting the folder aside.

"Susan," she said, after several silent bites, "what's going on?"

"Nothing right now."

"I don't get it," she said, putting her plate to one side with less than half the sandwich eaten. I quietly finished mine. "We find out this really interesting stuff from Roz, and you hardly spoke to her. You didn't ask a single question. Now you have another lead, and when I call, you hide in the bedroom. And you never did tell me about the hallucination, or how that shopkeeper knew your name." Her eyes were pinning me to the bed. I felt trapped, helpless, but as usual when caught that way, I could think quickly, if not well.

"That's the shop I told you about, the one where I got the scrapbook," I said.

41

Her eyebrows knit together into a frown. She had a memory for detail.

"You said that shop was downtown," she remembered. "I'd hardly call that neighborhood downtown, even if it is ten blocks from here."

"I must have gotten confused," I stammered. "I went into a shop downtown also, but I bought the scrapbook up here."

She shook her head. "Susan, something's definitely wrong." She laid a hand on mine. "Maybe you should think about therapy again."

I could have predicted she would say that. She had been against my quitting therapy all along. She sided with my therapist, who claimed I wandered from degree to degree to please my mother, who was a highly regarded anthropology professor. I never bought the theory. "I don't need therapy," I snapped, "I need to go to sleep."

She sighed. "Letty King wasn't home, in case you're wondering. I guess I'll leave now," she said, in such a defeated voice, that I was immediately sorry I'd been curt.

"You don't have to go," I softened. I should have told her I knew she was trying to help, but that sometimes I felt like I was in a "Tough Love" program. Instead I said, "Here, I'm too tired to look through these clippings. Why don't we get into bed and you can read one to me?"

It was one of my favorite things to do. Catherine had a beautiful reading voice, full of expression.

"No, I should go," she insisted. At the door, she turned to me and looked like she was going to say something profound. "I—I'll call you," is what came out.

♦

The xeroxes of Sarah Stern's articles did not hold a lot of interest for me, but I scanned them anyway. First of all, reading a bad xerox is not quite the same as having the actual article, and secondly, they shed no light on her life with The Gang. But when I told Catherine about them the next day, she was almost beside herself with excitement.

"She witnessed the Triangle Shirtwaist fire!" she shouted into the phone. "And wrote about it! That's great!"

I was hesitant to admit I couldn't quite remember what the Triangle Shirtwaist fire was. I recalled the name, from an article Catherine had written in the feminist newspaper, but what it was exactly I couldn't put my finger on.

"Would you read it to me, Suze?" she asked. She only called me "Suze" when she wanted something or felt especially affectionate. I obliged.

EYEWITNESS TO MURDER

I was one of the lucky ones. There were one hundred and forty-six others who were not. They were mostly young immigrant women, of whom the management said, "Let 'em burn. They're a lot of cattle anyway." They jumped to their deaths or were swallowed up in the flames of the Triangle Shirtwaist Company on March 25, 1911.

I was a sewing machine operator for two years. It was not difficult work, but tedious, and the pay was $3.50 a week. I was there during the 1910 strike for better working conditions and was arrested twice for provoking policemen. We did get a shorter work week and a pay increase, but our work environment remained hazardous. Workroom doors were locked to prevent us from taking breaks. Sewing machines were jammed so close together, there was little room to move, and it was impossible to hear over the din. Bins in the cutting room were filled with scraps of flammable cotton and were not emptied for weeks. That Saturday afternoon, at quitting time, one of the cutters lit a cigarette.

Sarah's description of the fire was sickening. She had been fortunate enough to get pushed on to one of the elevators going down. On the street, she watched as her friends and co-workers plummeted to their deaths, so panicked by the encroaching flames they hurled themselves out of the windows to escape. The sidewalk was littered with bodies, some of whom she helped to identify.

My friend, Rachel Mikulsky, was barely recognizable. Like so many others, her dress had caught fire and had burned her badly. Her face was smashed from the fall to the sidewalk. This, I maintain, is nothing short of murder.

Catherine was quiet for a few moments. "This is great stuff," she finally said.

I knew what she meant. It was great for her, who had done so much research on immigrant women on the Lower East Side. But I wasn't quite sure what it told me.

"Do you mind if I do a little digging into Sarah Stern?" Catherine asked finally. "I didn't realize how interesting your Gang really is!"

I said I didn't mind, but that was just one more lie. I had the craziest feeling that Catherine was going to ruin everything.

♦

Maybe Catherine thought getting more involved would be helpful to me. Or maybe it was that she found something about The Gang that she could really hang on to. Or that it would be something for us to share. Whatever her rationale, and heedless of the fact that I didn't show a lot of interest, Catherine started bringing me things about Sarah Stern. How she found them is a mystery to me. I have never really understood how historians just seem to know where to find information.

"She was really prolific!" Catherine said, as she pulled out a manila envelope of xeroxed articles. "I haven't found anything earlier than that Triangle article, but after that, I guess she got political."

We were eating dinner at Catherine's, some unnamed dish she'd thrown together from various leftover takeout cartons. Whatever I had was a bizarre mixture of beef with broccoli and chicken in garlic sauce. I munched in silence.

"I'm really glad we talked to Roz, aren't you?" Catherine asked, poking a chopstick at the air for emphasis.

"I don't know," I answered.

Catherine looked at me quizzically. "What do you mean?"

"I mean, I'm not sure what all this stuff about the Triangle fire and labor organizing has to do with anything," I said.

"But this is the most interesting stuff!" she said, in surprise. I guess she was used to my agreeing with her. "I mean, look what a contribution this little-known woman was making. This makes those women come alive, almost like they're right here with us." She paused. "Don't you think?"

I looked around but saw no traces of Lucy or any of them, even Sarah. They had never felt deader to me than when reduced to some xeroxed articles.

"Listen to this," Catherine said eagerly, through a mouthful of something. "This is from Sarah's article about a mass feminist meeting at Cooper Union in 1914:

The spirit of fraternity and sorority filled the hall, and a cry went up from the crowd as Marie Jenny Howe stated the feminist agenda: "We're sick of being specialized to sex. We intend to be ourselves, not just our little female selves, but our whole, big, human selves."

I mean, can't you just see it all? Doesn't it make you want to be there?"

It did sound inspiring, but something in me remained unmoved. It occurred to me that all these things had to do with the public, not the private, Sarah. What was she like at home, with Elinor? Where did she and Lucy have dinner? What did they talk about when they were just being friends, just being The Gang, and not vociferous feminists?

This was not how I wanted to get to know the women in the photographs. The ones who winked at me and sent me postcards. Catherine was cluttering things up.

I got up abruptly, as she was reading another article, this

one about another garment factory strike, and picked up my knapsack.

"Hey," Catherine said, as I headed toward the door, "where are you going?"

"Home," I said, sadly. And in my mind I added, "To Lucy and Harriet."

♦ 7 ♦

I signed the lease for my apartment and asked Margielove if I could work full-time.

"I thought you were doing research and needed a flexible schedule."

"I need the money more," I said, and she looked into my eyes and saw, I guess, that she could believe me. I might stretch the truth about my hobbies and collections, but my nervousness about money must have shown through clearly.

"I see," she said.

She didn't have enough work for me full-time, so she gave me thirty hours a week and invited me to start collecting more things from the shop. That was how I began my collection of antiques from the 1920s. I figured that if I ever got too desperate, I could sell them on Broadway or at a flea market to pick up some cash. It was a nice assortment of pressed glass, mechanical toys, magazines, china, women's costume accessories, and some odd bits of furniture. Oh, and always, of course, books and photographs.

My apartment, which was small to begin with, began to take on the cluttered look of a rotting old historical society. "How can you afford this stuff?" Catherine asked me. We were seeing less of each other, and each time she came over, I had two or three new things.

"The woman at Out of Time gives me a good deal," I said, somewhat truthfully.

After that night at her apartment, Catherine stopped asking me about my research. If she was doing any more of her own, which I doubt, she didn't mention it. In fact, she stopped asking me about most things. She was really angry at me and had to keep herself from exploding several times. Part of me wanted to explain. Twice I almost told her I had quit Columbia, but I stopped short at the crucial moment. "Catherine, there's something I want to tell you. I've quit —" and the look of worry in her eyes made me hesitate. So I had to cut down on two of my minor vices, just so I wouldn't have to lie to her again.

"— drinking," I finished once, and she was very puzzled by the confession.

"You hardly drink at all," she said.

"And I don't like how I feel when I do," I insisted. "I'm going to try stopping for a while."

The second time, I finished with "— drinking so much coffee." I knew that would please Catherine, who drank nothing stronger than an occasional cup of Morning Thunder.

"That should help make you more relaxed," she observed, but the slight tilt of her chin and the slant of her left eyebrow made me think she knew I was bluffing.

I don't know why I alienated Catherine. It was as if I did it on purpose, to push her further and further away and to build a solid wall of lies between us. We'd been together three years, and sometimes it was hard to figure out why. She was brilliant and thoughtful, and I made her laugh. She said insightful things, and I listened well. She made suggestions, and I took them. Every now and then, I wondered where I had gone in the relationship. I depended so much on what Catherine thought of me. Now she was forging into my territory, taking over almost, and in a way I didn't like. Her fascination with precise facts and dates left no room for intuition or imagination. Or romance.

We had a big blowup after that evening at her place. She was furious with me, and said she was only trying to help. I repeated that the kind of help she had to offer wasn't really what I needed.

"Well, what do you need?" she said, hurt.

Embarrassed, I had to admit I didn't really know, what I

needed in general, or from her. I loved her, but I was beginning to love more the quick and unexpected sound of Harriet's laugh, the reassuring calm of Lucy's voice. "Trust yourself," Lucy had told me, and ultimately I did just that. It was the best advice I'd had in a while. I trusted that something special was happening to me, and that I was not just going crazy.

◆

I woke up one morning with the touch of soft, warm lips on mine. At first, I didn't know they were lips. I thought maybe a butterfly had fluttered against my cheeks and landed on my mouth. I reached up dreamily to brush it off, and realized it was a kiss instead.

"That's what a kiss was like in 1926," someone said, and the honeyed tone told me that it was Harriet.

◆

Out of Time was beginning to take on a new look. After weeks of arranging the books and postcards, I took on the harder task of everything else, the mountains of stuff piled in the middle of the room and overflowing out to the edges. Broken furniture and china we put out onto the street as part of our community service project. One day as I walked up Broadway, I saw a street vendor using one of our chairs. He had improvised a broken broom handle for the fourth leg. Another day I saw one of our battered end tables and broken dishes being used by a homeless woman to eat her lunch, the remainders of someone's Big Mac and Filet o' Fish. The project, I reported to Margielove, was working well.

We were becoming good friends. She tolerated me in a way others never had, not even Catherine. Catherine, I sometimes thought, loved me for what I might become. But Margielove had a true affection for me as I was.

"Van Dine," she would say when I showed up for work. She started to call me by my last name as we became more familiar. "Look at the great piece of junk I found for you." She saved all the twenties stuff for me and gave me first dibs on all of it. People would come into the store looking for items from the twenties, cookware or glasses or jewelry, and she steered them away. "No twenties stuff here," she scowled. "I can't stand the hullabaloo around the twenties." The customers looked confused until she pointed them down Broadway, to another shop. "They have better stuff," she said.

She was not much of a businesswoman, and she did not really like antiques that much. The reason the place got straightened up in just a little over a month was that she never bought any new merchandise. We simply kept selling off, slowly, what she acquired when she bought the store. After I cleaned out the center of the store, we brought things up from the basement. Soon there was nothing down there but some rusty metal shelves. I wondered what we'd do when we sold everything. I asked her.

"Go to Bermuda?" she suggested.

As the summer wore on, there was less and less to straighten up, and I convinced Margielove that it was good business to purchase more inventory. As long as she didn't have to do it, she didn't care. She paid me to comb the classifieds for estate sales and flea markets. But the items were already marked up so high, we would have had to inflate the prices beyond reason to make a profit.

"You have to go out of New York," I said, frustrated. "It's like the rents, everything's too outrageously overpriced here."

"Why don't you then?" she said casually.

"Why don't I then what?" I asked.

"Go out of New York." She was eating a salt bagel oozing with cream cheese.

I shook my head. "I'd need a car," I said, "and cash."

"We have both," she said, explaining that she had an old station wagon parked in New Jersey that she never used because it was too tight for her behind the wheel. The store's account was doing well; we had sold a lot by making the store more presentable. But we would have a problem soon if she didn't either sell the store or get more merchandise.

"I don't care which way we go," she said, making it my decision. I had gone, in a short time, from part-time employee to management consultant. "What do you think?"

I needed the job. I wanted the job. And I seemed to have nothing holding me in New York, now that Catherine and I were on the rocks.

"I could go upstate," I said with a glimmer in my eye. "To Saratoga and Glens Falls."

"Whatever," she said, licking the cream cheese from her thumb.

◆

When I told Catherine I needed to get away before fall term, she sounded almost relieved. We had been bickering a lot. When I said I was going upstate to do some research, she really perked up, probably hoping I was finally getting my act together.

"That's terrific," she said. I could see her smiling even over the phone. "I'm so glad you're following through on this." There was a fumble of hesitation from her end. "Can I — can I see you before you go?" she asked. "Maybe I could make dinner."

I knew what Catherine's dinners were. They were my favorite meals, lovingly prepared, usually from Marcella Hazan's *Classic Italian Cookbook*. They were invariably served by candlelight, with some flowers and an appropriate wine. They were often eaten in the nude, after an hour or two of sex. They didn't happen that frequently, but when they did they managed to cement our relationship, at least temporarily, until the memory had worn off. They were usually followed by more sex, elaborate and carried on till early morning.

"Of course," I said, the anticipation both painful and pleasurable at the same time. "I'd like that."

◆

The morning I left to drive upstate, Catherine turned toward me in bed and took my face in her hands.

"Look," she said, and I had no choice but to stare into the infinity of those green eyes, "I don't know what's going on with you, and you obviously don't want me to know. I don't know what's going on with us either."

I started to answer, to say something vaguely reassuring, but she pushed both her thumbs lightly across my lips.

"But if last night is any indication of what we feel for each other, I think we have something worth working out." She moved her thumbs and kissed me straight on. Our eyes locked. "Come back to me," she demanded simply.

She rolled on top of me then and took one of my breasts firmly in her mouth. The rest, shall we say, is history.

In the end, I was gone less than a week, but it felt like much longer. I followed the Hudson River and stayed away, as much as possible, from the interstates. I wanted the opportunity to stop whenever I saw a yard sale or a junk store.

I have never known much about antiques. I was not the best choice to send on a buying trip. Within the first day, I filled a few boxes with Depression glass and imitation Fiestaware. One good find just north of Kingston was a porch sale full of pressed back chairs, most in good condition, just needing some refinishing. I bought the lot of them and sand-wiched them tightly into the back of the station wagon.

In New York, by this time in my shopping, the car would have been sliced open to get whatever potentially valuable stuff was inside. Upstate, I sometimes left the car unlocked. The further north I got, the more relaxed I felt, like New York City was just a bad memory.

The most valuable things I brought along were pictures of The Gang. I couldn't see traveling without them, not to the area where Lucy was born and Harriet had her first dramatic success. The closer I came to Saratoga Springs, the stronger I felt their presence. In fact, I thought someone said, "Oh, look!" a few times on the road outside of town, but I didn't recognize the voice.

I had never been to Saratoga Springs, and it struck me as a little jewel of the North Country. I knew immediately I wanted to stay at The Saratoga House, which had not changed appreciably in one hundred years. It was not in my budget; camping and cheap bed and breakfasts were. But it sat so invitingly on Broadway at the beginning of a line of perfectly preserved old buildings, I was pulling out my credit card before I realized what I was doing.

"It's worth the expense," someone behind me whispered in a familiar voice. I turned quickly, expecting to see Harriet, but a middle-aged couple in tourists' clothes stood behind me.

"Excuse me?" I said.

"I said, it's worth the expense," the woman repeated, in a different accent altogether, a New England twang. "We've stayed here twice before. You'll love it."

I don't know how she knew I was concerned about money, but I vaguely remember echoing the price of a single room twice after the concierge told me.

All the way up to the room, I kept thinking how foolish I was, spending money I didn't have and would be paying back for months. I kept thinking, I should be on my way to do my job, further north, where the bargains would be even better. I kept thinking, don't do this, don't turn the key in the lock, don't establish yourself in the oak bed, don't linger at the window pretending you're in another time. But then I was there already, and there didn't seem to be much sense in turning back.

◆

The bed was smaller than average, a three-quarter size not quite big enough for two but more than adequate for one. The headboard and footboard were elaborately carved with rows of beading and flowers. There were a simple oak dresser and wash stand to match. I had seen drawings of similar bedroom suites in an old Sears Roebuck catalog Margielove had at the store to help date our kitchen utensils. In 1912, the set had cost about forty dollars.

Now I was lying in the bed, thinking about all the people who had had sex there, conceived children there, maybe even died there. For all I knew, this could have been the very room Lucy and Harriet had had in Saratoga when Harriet had her success in *Miss Morley*, the very bed in which they celebrated her new career. Before I dozed off, I thought about the dream I had in which Lucy and Harriet were making love in a rosewood bed, and it lulled me happily to sleep.

I woke with a start, probably from some noise out in the street, and tried to keep my heavy eyelids open. A deep shaft of afternoon sun cut across the floor like a spotlight. The slant of it was disorienting. In the pool of light it left at the foot of the bed stood Harriet.

"Actually, it's two flights down," she said.

"What?" I asked, rubbing my eyes and propping myself up on my elbows.

"Our room," she answered simply, as if I should have known, as if I had just asked a question and she was politely responding. "When we stay here, we always stay in the third-floor corner room that looks up Broadway. That way," she laughed, her high, fruity laugh, "I can say I've made it to Broadway."

"Did you ever?" I ventured carefully, as she watched me from behind long, lazy lashes.

"In a manner of speaking," she said, laughing again. This time the laugh had a little catch in it, like a hiccup. "But we don't need to talk about that now." Her voice became lower, softer, more alluring. "Lucy's asleep."

In the moment before she came to me on the bed, when she was undoing the pearly buttons of her blouse and dropping her skirt to the floor, something occurred to me that hadn't before. I said it aloud.

"Not really," she answered, "but she's faithful to me."

She left on her cream silk teddy. She looked different close up, prettier, but less fragile. Her mouth tasted like melted chocolate and brandy. Her skin smelled like fresh cut roses. Her heart pounded just like mine. Her hands on my breasts were familiar. In between kisses I managed to say, "But Lucy. And Catherine." Harriet swallowed the words right out of my mouth.

"It's for your education," she purred, her tongue exploring the curves of my ear. "Tell yourself it's for history."

55

♦

When I woke up, the air in the room was cold. I was shivering under the bed covers, fully clothed, even in my shoes. The window was open, the sun was just going down. My left shoulder ached, my back was stiff, and my mouth tasted like stale liquor. I tried to recall if I'd been drinking, then I remembered that I'd given up what little I drank weeks before. I decided I should start again.

I had locked the door from the inside and it was still locked. I tugged at it two or three times to reassure myself. Everything in the room looked the same, but different, too. In the shadows of sunset the wood was darker, richer, the wallpaper had more flowers in it, the ceiling was just a little bit lower. I rifled through my bag for the handful of pictures I'd brought with me. I wanted to see if there was anything different about Harriet's smile.

But they were gone. I knew it in the instant I unzipped the bag. I pulled everything out of it twice. I checked in pockets, underwear, in every page of the book I was reading. I combed the floor on my hands and knees. I inspected every drawer, every crevice of the armchair. I even unmade the bed and flipped over the mattress. Then I picked up the phone to call the front desk.

"There's been a theft," I planned to say, "of some valuable photographs. From my room as I slept. I left the window open. Nothing else seems to be missing."

But when the concierge answered, I merely asked, "How late is the dining room open?"

Then I took a shower and changed my clothes, scolding myself for being so naive, so trustworthy. I had no reason to believe that a flapper from the 1920s wouldn't do me wrong.

"But Harriet," I said incredulously. Then her face came back to me from the photos, the teasing slant of her hat, the suggestive tilt of her eyebrow, the knowing part of her lips.

"*Especially* Harriet," I decided. Suddenly it all seemed like a game: the clues, the appearances, the hints and suggestions, and finally the theft, or borrowing, of the pictures. It was a game, I realized, that could go on forever. I could play, as I had been, or not. I could force them to tell me their story; I could try to learn the story myself. Who was to say, anyway, that they would tell me correctly, especially Harriet, who was false to me and Lucy? I repacked my bag and carried it down to the front desk.

The concierge was surprised that I was checking out at seven p.m., not having spent the night.

"I needed a nap," I said, "and to freshen up." It was something you might do at a fifteen-dollar-a-night motel, but not what this hotel was accustomed to.

"Tell me," I said, as he was accepting my keys, "the room at the corner on the third floor, facing up Broadway?"

"Facing north? Yes?" He looked at me skeptically, as if he would not have been surprised if I wanted to check back in.

"Is anyone in that room now?"

He perused his records. "No," he said.

"Do you suppose I could see it?" I asked, signing the final bill. "My parents stayed there on their honeymoon. It has, you know, memories."

"Well," he said, "that would be highly unusual." He bit his bottom lip. He was not cold, just cautious.

He had a bellhop take me to the room. The boy hardly said a word. He barely looked at me. He must have thought, here's another crazy tourist. Or else he had sized me up and was anticipating no tip.

The room was larger than mine had been, almost a suite, with two of everything — two windows, two chairs, two dressers, two nightstands. The wallpaper was rose with two thin alternating stripes of white and deep green. The lithographs on the wall, all of old Saratoga, were hung in two's. There were two green cotton area rugs on the hardwood floor.

Between the twin nightstands stood a huge rosewood sleigh bed, the bed in my dreams.

"Has that always been here?" I asked.

"I dunno," the boy said. "Since I've been here."

"How long is that?"

"Since last Christmas." He started to shift impatiently

57

from one foot to the other. "The manager would know, I guess."

I took two one-dollar bills out of my wallet, folded them up, and handed them to him. "It doesn't matter," I said. I took one final look around the room while he uncrinkled the bills. I walked to the window and stared up Broadway, I touched the windowsill just as others had, hundreds of times before. I pressed my nose to the cool glass, then wiped the smudge it left there with my sleeve.

"I have to get back to work now, ma'am," he reminded me.

"Of course," I said, fingering the wallpaper lightly on my way out. At the full-length mirror near the door, I stopped to inspect the worn marks in the floorboards, contemplating the shuffling of feet over time as people on their way out to dinner, the theater, the racetrack, took one last assessment of their looks. I looked tired.

The mirror caught the corner of the bed, where Harriet sat. I turned to her to ask where my pictures were, just as the bellhop flipped off the light.

"Oh, sorry," he said. "I thought you were done." When the light clicked on again, Harriet was gone.

"I am," I said, closing the door behind me.

♦

By that time it was too dark to pitch a camp, so I drove back to one of the cheap tourist motels I passed on my way into town. There I had what they called a cabin, which was really nothing more than a double bed surrounded by four walls. One of the four walls was shared with another half of the cabin. I was kept awake most of the night by moans and crashing bedsprings on the other side of that wall. The rest of the night, I tossed and tumbled on a mattress that had seen better days. No matter where I started out, I ended up rolling to the middle.

In the morning, when I got into my car, things inside

looked different, but just slightly so, like the time my apartment was robbed by a considerate burglar who closed all the drawers and locked the door on his way out. It took a while to figure out something was wrong. In the back of the car, I did a quick visual inventory and everything seemed to be in place. Then I sniffed roses in the air.

On the floor of the front passenger seat was the packet of photos, as if they'd been hiding there all along. They were all there, but with one more added, one I hadn't seen before. It was a picture of Harriet, sitting in a chair in the suite I'd just visited, surrounded by roses. She held a handmade sign in front of her that read "Harriet on Broadway." As always, her eyebrow was cocked, and her lips curled deliciously into a smile.

♦

On the road to Glens Falls, I remembered why I was making this trip and stopped several times at run-down antiques and thrift stores. I picked up some old dime novels and a couple of printer's type trays for next to nothing. At a yard sale just south of Glens Falls, I found a collection of nice old wooden planes that had belonged to the owner's grandfather.

"What will you do with them?" he asked, following me to the car, where I had already tucked the box of planes out of sight.

"Display them," I said. It was only a lie of omission. I knew he wouldn't have sold them so readily to a dealer.

"Oh," he said, hovering near me, obviously unsure if he'd done the right thing. I was overcome by the memory of the antiques store downtown, the rain, the scrapbook, the guilt, the ethics of it all.

"Look," I said before I closed the back door, "if you'd like to change your mind, I'd understand. I mean, you can have them back."

"I was going to give them to the museum, y'know, but they couldn't pay me," he said distractedly. "My wife and me, we're moving to Florida and we can't take so much with us. And we need the cash." He held out his hand, and I shook it. "No," he smiled, "a deal's a deal."

"What was your grandfather's name?" I asked, writing it on the side of the box as he told me. "And his dates?" The word "dates" caught on my tongue. My lips tried to keep it in, but it snuck out anyway. With it came an overwhelming loneliness for Catherine.

"Born and raised not two miles from here," the man said.

"Well, I thank you for sharing this part of your history," I said with a full, off-white smile, the one I reserve for my best days.

He gave me a half-salute as I drove away. I had already decided to give the planes to the museum in Glens Falls. In some small way, I had to atone for the scrapbook.

◆ 9 ◆

Letty King lived in a rambling white house not unlike all the others in Glens Falls. The town was immaculately middle-class. From what I could see, there was no bad part of town, no wrong side of the tracks. What seemed to be the slightly poorer neighborhood was still pristine, just a little more crowded. The town looked like a set for a Thornton Wilder play. It made me suddenly homesick for the diversity and dishevelment of Manhattan.

It's hard to believe I went there uninvited, unannounced, and harder to believe that Letty King didn't keep me on the other side of the screen door. She did not at all appreciate the mention of her aunt's name.

"My aunt Lucy!" she shrilled. "My aunt Lucy! What's all this sudden fascination with my aunt Lucy! First, a call from that archivist from New York City, now you. You'd think she was *famous* or something!"

I explained, or at least gave my white-washed version, of how I happened on the scrapbook. I pulled out the photos for her to see.

She shrieked when she saw them, and held a hand dramatically to her chest. She pushed the screen door open and waved me inside. "Let me see those," she demanded. She flipped through them hurriedly, wildly almost, ending up with the most recently acquired one of Harriet. "How did you get these?"

I had just told her, but Roz had warned me about her memory relapses. I repeated my story.

"Bea must have taken them," she mumbled.

"Excuse me?" I said. She wandered out of the foyer into the living room, probably furnished in the same way it had been for sixty years.

"Bea, my sister," she said, lowering herself heavily onto the camelback sofa. She didn't offer me a chair but I took one anyway, a small, narrow rocker with a caned seat.

"These pictures," she said, wiping a few beads of sweat from her nose, "belong to me."

I could not, in all honesty, protest and say, "Oh, no, I bought them fair and square." They felt like mine, but I knew all too well how I'd acquired them.

"How did you get them again?" and I related the story calmly, even though my stomach was churning.

"My sister Bea stole them from me," she said, angrily. "She must have come here and took them right out of the attic."

"Why would she do that?" I asked, as gently as I could.

"Because I wouldn't give them to her," she snapped. "She wanted the letters, too, and the diaries. She's afraid I'll burn them someday, like Mother wanted to. And maybe I will. But Aunt Lucy left them with Mother, and Mother left everything in this house to me. I can do what I like with them."

"They're so valuable, though," I said. Then, when her eyes brightened, I added quickly, "Historically speaking, that is."

She looked at me skeptically over her glasses. "You think so?"

"Oh, yes," I said. "There's a great demand to know what women's lives were like back then."

She snorted, "Well, she was hardly your typical woman. Maybe you don't know that."

"I know she was a lesbian," I said coolly. I thought I saw her shiver or maybe she just shifted in her seat.

"Yes, well," she said, obviously agitated.

"Of course, I'll give you back the pictures if you want," I gambled.

"Well, you bought them," she said, frowning. "If I'd

known they were worth something, I'd have sold them myself." She took off her glasses and wiped the sweat off the bridge of her nose. "What will you do with them?"

"I'd just like to look at them, study them," I said truthfully. "But I'd also like to find out more about all the women in them, which is why I'm here."

She handed the photos across to me. "And what would you give me for the rest?" she asked.

My heart was somewhere out of my chest, somewhere up past my throat, in my ears, beating till I couldn't hear myself talk. "The rest?" I asked meekly.

"The letters and other junk," she said. She pulled out a flowered cotton handkerchief and wiped her whole face several times. "There's a big box of it upstairs."

I couldn't think quickly enough. "Oh, it's so hard to put a price tag on history," I said. "Maybe a hundred dollars?"

She laughed out loud and pushed herself up from the sofa. "You just said it was valuable. That's what you call valuable?" She started to walk out into the foyer, and I watched her go while I clutched the photos. At the doorway, she glanced back over her shoulder at me. "Well, come on then," she said impatiently. "Don't you want to see it?"

I scrambled up from the little chair with difficulty, almost tipping it over frontwards as I did. She led me up two flights to a door that hid a steeper, more narrow staircase, bathed in light from dormer windows. The third floor of the house was set up as a small apartment. The ceilings were lower than downstairs, and there were numerous charming eaves. There was an efficiency kitchen, a bedroom with a large iron bed, and a bright living room with wicker furniture. The bathroom was reigned by a footed bathtub, which the whole Gang probably would have fit into comfortably.

"Who lives here?" I asked, imagining myself entertaining company in the huge bathtub.

"No one now," she said. "Aunt Lucy did briefly, when I was a girl. She had a bit of a breakdown and stayed here for a few months. When I got older, before I married King, Mother let me move up here. Then, later, Mother turned the rest of the house over to me and King, and she made the third floor home. That's when we put in the efficiency kitchen."

"Lucy had a breakdown?" I asked, my heartbeats drowning out my voice again. "I can't believe it."

Letty looked suddenly skeptical, her memory clearly not all it once was. "Yes, yes, I think so," she hesitated. "At least I thought so."

"Then I'm sure she did," I added, reassuringly.

"When what's-her-name died," she muttered. "That friend of hers. The little flirt, what was her name again?"

For me, the air had gotten thicker at the word "died." The sun had become unbearably bright. It reflected off the windows in blinding strokes. It made me suddenly too tired to stand.

"Harriet," I said, wearily.

"Yes, that's it," she agreed.

She was already pulling a big box out of the closet on the landing. The cardboard looked like it would give way under her tugging, but I didn't offer to help. I had dropped into one of the kitchen chairs.

"This is it," she said. "Letters, some diaries, some mementos, the manuscripts of some stories she wrote. Mother wanted to get rid of it years ago, but Bea stopped her. This is worth more than, what did you say? Two hundred dollars?"

I nodded and reached over into the box. Bunches of letters tied up with ribbon. Some Moroccan leather notebooks, well worn. Large brown packages neatly wrapped. All precisely packed away. For history.

"Who did this?" I asked. "Who organized the box?"

She looked puzzled. "Why, Aunt Lucy, I guess," she said. "Mother wouldn't have bothered. Don't you want to inspect the stuff? After all, three hundred is a lot of money for a bunch of paper. You *did* say three hundred?"

I nodded again.

"Actually, I bet it's worth three thousand," she said. "I bet some museum would give me three thousand dollars."

I stood up, my knees weak. It was very hot and stuffy in the attic. "I have to go now," I said. "I'm sorry to have taken your time. I don't have three thousand dollars. I was just hoping you'd let me read the stuff. Just for curiosity's sake."

I started down the stairs, where I could feel the cool air circulating from the second floor. I breathed it in deeply and felt instantly clearer headed.

"Wait a minute," she called after me. "Can you come back tomorrow? Tomorrow at one."

"What for?" I asked.

"Just come back," she said, and not knowing why but having nothing to lose, I did.

◆

From the sidewalk I could see the cardboard box on the porch, waiting for me. Letty King sat next to it on the porch glider.

"I bet you thought I'd forget," she said, without saying hello.

The thought had crossed my mind, but I didn't say so. "Hello, Mrs. King."

"I called my son to get it down from the attic," she said. "But you'll have to get it into your car."

I gulped. "But, Mrs. King, I told you I don't have three thousand dollars."

"That's the problem with you people," she said, but she didn't say what the problem was or which people she meant. "It's worthless. Worthless junk. Library doesn't want any queer letters. They'll rot in my attic. My son could care less about them. So go ahead, get them out of here. I'll be glad to be rid of them. Save me the trouble of throwing them out."

I hesitated, one foot on the porch, the other on the steps ready to beat a retreat. "And what about your sister?" I asked.

"Haven't seen her since 1967," she said. "You tell her. . . you tell her she owes me a few Christmas presents."

I reached over and touched the side of the box timidly. There was a perfect spot for it in the car right in the back. If I'd bought any more inventory, it wouldn't have fit. I could see it there now, riding comfortably back to Manhattan. I could hear myself calling Catherine to tell her the news. I could see my renewed self-confidence mirrored in her eyes.

And I could suddenly picture the antiques shop downtown and a woman with salt-and-pepper hair arranging marcasite pins.

"I'd feel better," I said, "if you asked her first if she wants the box." I couldn't believe I was saying it. I knew she would want it. Maybe she would send me bits of it in the mail, but she would want it just the same.

"You ask her," Letty said gruffly. "Now get it out of here before somebody sets a match to it."

I grabbed two neighborhood kids and paid them two bucks each to help me carry the box to the car. There was not another inch of room in the back of the station wagon, so I would start for home that day and not bother heading further north, as I had planned.

Letty was still in the porch glider, watching. I waved to her as I closed the back door. "A perfect fit!" I shouted but she didn't respond. I walked back to the porch, and she examined every step I took.

"Thank you," I said simply.

"Don't ever use my name," she said.

"Excuse me?"

She stood up and smoothed her housedress. She patted her hair into place, even though I hadn't noticed a wisp of it move.

"If you write something about her, don't ever use my name," she said, more loudly and slowly, as if she thought I had a hearing impairment. "Letitia Best King. I'll sue you if you do."

"Maybe we should sign an agreement," I said, handing her a check for a hundred dollars, the original price I offered. She took it with some surprise and shoved it roughly into her pocket.

"Just don't use it," she repeated.

I turned to go but had one last question. "Your sister Bea," I said. "What's her last name? So I can contact her."

Letty laughed shrilly. "Don't ask me," she said. "It used to

66

be Best. But I haven't heard from her since 1967. Did I tell you that?"

I nodded.

"She could be married for all I know. She could be queer, too. For all I know." She opened the screen door and it clacked noisily closed behind her. The front door shut firmly right after her.

I sat down heavily on the porch steps. I could feel Letty's eyes through the window. I could feel the moist heat of approaching August. I could feel the weight of history on my shoulders.

Pretty soon I was driving south, out of town, toward Saratoga again. I was picking up speed, then slamming to a stop in front of a familiar house. I had a sheet of paper to give to the man on the porch, who was cleaning up the last traces of his yard sale. It was from the museum in Glens Falls. It acknowledged the gift of a collection of valuable wooden planes. The look on his face helped me endure the drive ahead.

✦ 10 ✦

I would have gotten into Manhattan late with nowhere to put the car and the stuff in it, so I ended up staying overnight at a campground outside New Paltz. I guess it was stupid not to stay in Saratoga, but the whole town made me feel manipulated and dishonest. The concern that Catherine would know I'd been unfaithful shot back and forth through my head all night, keeping me awake. We'd had a lot of discussions about monogamy versus nonmonogamy, and Catherine had made a strong case that the latter worked better in theory than in practice. So far, we hadn't had reason to test our fidelity to each other. Catherine found it easier to be monogamous, because she was so busy, and I'd never entertained the thought of anyone else since we'd met. Till now.

Maybe my restlessness was from the realization that I could never expunge myself of the guilt, because to do so would expose the crazy, inexplicable turn my life had taken. Or possibly it was just because I'd arrived too late again to make camp and had to deal with the discomfort of sitting upright in my car all night, with my mummy bag tucked around me in an unnatural way. I was suddenly afraid to get into it, afraid that this would be the time the zipper would break and I'd be locked in my car in a mummy bag. I realized later that my paranoia had gotten stronger the closer I came to Manhattan.

I drove into the city in mid-morning, straight to Out of Time to unload the car. I hadn't washed my hair in several days and my mouth felt gummy, but I was anxious for

Margielove to see my purchases and knew they wouldn't last long in a parked car in Manhattan.

The store was closed. The gates were locked. Inside, the shop looked like it had not been open for a while. The merchandise had an appearance of neglect and sadness. I didn't know what to think.

I had keys, so I unpacked the car alone, as quickly as I could. As it was, I lost a few items to kids on the street, but that felt to me like more community service. I left the box of Lucy's papers in the back and ripped the cardboard so thieves could see it was filled with things they wouldn't want. Then I made a call to Margielove's apartment.

It rang ten times, maybe more. I dialed again, and this time it rang fifteen. A third time it rang twenty.

I got back into the car and drove to her studio apartment on Seventy-ninth Street. She lived above a restaurant, with the neon sign from it shining directly into her front window, just like in cheap hotels in the movies. For the privilege she paid six hundred dollars a month.

I buzzed a dozen times. I banged on the inside door. A neighbor came out of an apartment and told me she was calling the cops. "Where's Margielove?" I shouted through the glass.

"Who?" she must have said, but all I could see were her lips forming a small, puckered "o."

"Marjorie," I screamed again. "Marjorie. Marjorie." It was at that moment I realized I didn't know her last name. It had never seemed important. She always paid me in cash, so I didn't even have a check with her signature. "Wait a minute," I yelled. "Please, one minute."

I raced out to the car, where I tore through the glove compartment for her registration. I couldn't find anything but a stack of Baskin-Robbins napkins and some receipts from the George Washington Bridge.

"I don't know her last name," I pleaded. "She's a big woman. Dresses in bright colors. She lives in 3R."

"Oh, her," the woman said, still not opening up the door, but talking more loudly so I could hear the muffled words, like someone talking through a blanket. "She hasn't been around. I thought she was away."

It must have been exhaustion that kept me from going to the police. I went home instead, struggling with the box, pulling it behind me onto the elevator, almost leaving half the contents strewn through the lobby of my building. Inside, I collapsed on the sofa and ripped off my clothes to cool down. I played back the messages on my answering machine and listened to a strange man named Arthur Harris urgently asking me to call him. And then to Catherine's impatient voice asking me to call her. And then to a series of hang-ups and a message in Spanish I couldn't understand. I fell asleep and didn't call anyone. I dreamt that Margielove had died. I dreamt that Lucy was running the shop. I dreamt that Catherine was very angry with me. And then I woke up, with the phone in my hand.

◆

It was all sort of true. Actually, some of it was truer than the rest of it. The truest thing, and the most horrifying, was that Margielove was indeed dead.

It was a typical New York accident. On her way to work, Margielove looked carefully down Broadway, waiting for traffic to break, then she crossed and was struck from the other direction by someone on a bike who never stopped. Probably had an urgent envelope to deliver to midtown, couldn't take the time to help the woman he'd just flattened. The doctor at St. Luke's Hospital had said it wasn't the impact that killed her, it was the shock that started her cardiac arrest. She died before the EMS arrived, died right in the middle of Broadway, on the island there, where some other pedestrians had pulled her so she wouldn't get hit again by an errant taxicab. The old people gave up their bench for her, and she lay there and died. I would like to say she never knew what hit her, but that doesn't seem to be true. She had a pretty good idea.

I probably would never have known this if she hadn't had a lawyer. He was Arthur Harris from my answering machine.

When he couldn't reach me, he called Catherine. I'd given her phone number to Margielove as a way to reach me in an emergency. When I woke up with the phone to my ear, Catherine was relating the story on the other end. There was just enough anger in her voice to wake me up.

"Who is this woman?" Catherine demanded. "The lawyer said she was your employer. I didn't argue with him. I knew there must be some good explanation." She paused for a deep breath and for a response from me. "Is there?" she asked.

"She's my employer," I said. "She *was* my employer."

Catherine was quiet again and extraordinarily patient, given the circumstances. "I guess you know," she said, "I haven't a clue to what's going on here." She cleared her throat. "I mean, when did you take a job? And why... why in the world has this woman named you in her will?"

It was too many questions. I couldn't remember when I'd taken the job. It seemed like a very long time ago, or no time at all. I started crying softly into the receiver. It was so unlike me that Catherine got scared. I guess it was that. Because she left school early that day and came straight to my apartment. I started crying again the minute she arrived.

♦

It was hard to get Catherine to talk after I told her the truth about school. She faced me across the coffee table like a stone carving. Knowing something is up is very different from knowing what that something is. The extent of my lying became apparent to both of us. If it shocked me how devious I'd been, I can imagine how Catherine felt.

I didn't have to imagine, she expressed it.

"Well," she said, her voice catching on the soft roll of the "l's," "I can see what our relationship means to you."

"It means a lot," I said, but knew she had no reason to believe me. "I love you, Catherine."

"All the lies," she said, shaking her head. "It's worse than being unfaithful."

I looked away. I thought I could never explain my unfaithfulness, too. Then she would think I was crazy.

"I don't understand why you had to lie so much," the stone carving said. Catherine, I felt, had left the room.

And Harriet had entered it. I could hear her voice faintly from the kitchen alcove. "You can get her back," she said. "Believe me. Just tell her everything."

It seemed like sound advice, even considering that it came from Harriet. For that moment, I was sure that Catherine Synge, the historian of women, could forgive me anything if she knew the whole truth.

"I wish I hadn't," I said. "I wish I'd been honest from the beginning. If you'll listen now, I'll tell you everything."

Catherine swallowed back her anger and disappointment. "It better be good," she said.

"Catherine," I said, "I'm having this historical experience." And by the look on her face, which softened from stone while I told the story, she must have thought it was pretty good indeed.

◆

Margielove had left me everything. The store on Broadway, plus all of its inventory and cash. Her car. The contents of her apartment. Her checking account. Her savings account. Her CDs. I was the beneficiary of her generous life insurance policy. I went overnight from worrying how I would pay my rent each month to being well off. I could stop spending a dollar twice a week on Lotto.

After she was dead, it became clear that I had been her only real friend. She'd talked about other friends, people who died of drug overdoses in the sixties or who wiped out on motorcycles in the seventies. But she had no one in her life in the eighties. It explained why she smiled at me sometimes for no reason, why she liked to stand behind the counter and watch me sort silver spoons. I don't think she was in love with me, but was just as genuinely fond of me as I was of her. Every now and then, I caught her looking at me and she gave me a thumbs up or the peace sign. Now I didn't know what I'd do without her.

"I walked into a store, looking for spoons," I told people, which was not true, but made a good story, "and I ended up with a business and a pile of money."

I didn't know then where she got her money, how an ex-hippie had amassed a business and about 250,000 dollars in cash. Maybe someone had left it to her. Maybe she had made it selling drugs. I didn't want to know. I decided I would just pay off my loans, live well, and revere her memory.

She had left instructions with her attorney for a cremation and a modest service. We held the ceremony at her apartment, with "Sgt. Pepper" as the background music and a few straggly-looking bums as guests, who may have been her friends or may have been just street people looking for a free meal. We served coffee and junk food, mostly Twinkies, her favorite snack. Then Catherine and I packed her urn into the station wagon and drove upstate to Bethel, where we scattered her ashes in the field where the Woodstock concert had taken place. Then, in her honor, we spent the rest of the day browsing through antiques and junk shops. We bought a lot of silly stuff, like Beatle bubble gum cards and a John Kennedy bottle opener, before we headed back to New York, popping beers with our new purchase. Margielove, I know, would have liked it.

◆ 11 ◆

After I moved in Margielove's things, my apartment looked like a junk store run by an eclectic collector who couldn't decide if she wanted to live in the 1920s, the 1960s, or the present. But I felt I owed it to her to keep everything intact. I knew she'd left her possessions to me because I wouldn't sell them, but would either keep them or give them away to street people. I decided to live with all of it for a while, a big jumble of the twentieth century, because I was feeling a bit lost without Margielove at work.

I also decided to keep the store. I never really pictured myself as a shopkeeper. I assumed I'd be a novelist or a great literary scholar or both. I think it was something in Catherine's voice that made me suddenly think I could run a store. She went with me, the weekend after Margielove's cremation, to get the store ready to reopen. We unpacked all the merchandise I'd brought from upstate, dated and priced it. Catherine feather-dusted everything, because for some reason, though the place had been sealed like a tomb for two weeks, there was a fine layer of soot over everything.

"Must have been in the air," I said. "New York's so filthy."

I was standing behind the counter, just as Margielove always had, trying to acquaint myself with her bookkeeping system, when I glanced up and saw Catherine watching me fondly as she brushed the tops of things with her duster.

"You look good there," she said. "You look at home, like you like what you're doing."

And I had to admit I did. Maybe, I thought, maybe that M.B.A. wasn't such a useless degree after all.

"Have you decided what to do?" she asked later, as we were sitting on two of the pressed back chairs from upstate, splitting a turkey sandwich. "Do you think you'll keep this place?"

I watched her admiringly as she leaned into her sandwich, so neat and careful. Catherine, unlike most people I knew, never got a stray drop of mayonnaise on her mouth, never left shreds of turkey in the paper wrapping.

"I like the idea of it," I said. "But whether or not I'd be successful is another story. Small businesses fail all the time in New York. And they're hard work. I'd never have time for anything else. Well, not that I *do* much of anything else, but if I was able to start writing again, there wouldn't be time."

"If you don't do this," she asked, after her last bite, "what would you do?"

"Go back to school," I said. "I guess."

We looked at each other. I saw the smiling curve of my own mouth mirrored in hers. We were simultaneously thinking of my stacked up diplomas, my restless wandering from university to university, my hasty retreat from Columbia.

"Well," Catherine said, "I guess that settles it."

◆

Out of Time reopened on the following Monday, and business was about as slow as I'd ever seen it. Of course, it was raining, and things always move more slowly in the rain. I used the long lulls between customers to go through the ledgers again and to create a system that worked better than the one Margielove had used. If the auditors came to call, I wanted to be ready.

It rained all week, one of those endless grey spans of time that New York is famous for. Each day was darker than the last. At the end of the week, at midday, it was so dark it looked as if someone had turned off the sun. There was a sudden fierce thunderstorm that made the lights in the store flicker a few times, then go out altogether. I went cautiously to the front door and locked it, tripping over a few baskets of things and the edge of the carpet.

I heard a noise from the corner of the store, near the books, or maybe it was just my mind playing tricks on me. I groped behind the counter for a flashlight whose batteries were weak from disuse, and I sent a thin, eerie shaft of light toward the back of the store. There was nothing there, but it looked like some books had fallen over on a shelf. I went to investigate, my flashlight getting dimmer and dimmer until it only afforded me a small yellow dot of light. I shined it on the shelf where a book had collapsed onto its front cover, with others tumbling over in a domino fashion. I pushed them all upright, setting the culprit, which was called *Central Park*, slightly tilted to hold the rest in place. I didn't bother to look at it further; I'd seen sentimental novels of the early 1900s many times before, always with names like *Central Park* or *On Fifth Avenue*. Just as my flashlight was fading for good, the lights of the store flickered on and off again, then on to stay. The rain had let up a little.

I went to unlock the door. An older man whose umbrella had been turned inside out was huddled in the doorway under the awning. I urged him in out of the storm.

"I thought you were closed," he said.

"No, temporary power failure. I locked up just to be safe," I explained.

He asked if I had any old umbrellas for sale, and I happened to have a few with broken ribs that would keep him at least partially dry. I guess they were Margielove's, though they looked too small to cover her. I gave him one for free.

"Gee, thanks," he said, as surprised as I probably would have been to get something for free in New York. He must have felt obliged to browse through the store, because he stayed quite a while.

Eventually, the rain became a soft drizzle and my customer came to the counter with three books. One of them was *Central Park*.

"I collect things about the city," he said, when I turned it over, looking for the price. "Souvenirs, books, postcards. You had more books than I usually find in one place."

I opened up *Central Park*, still looking for the price. I was about to give up and charge him fifty cents, like the others, when the title page flipped open in my hand. And the author's name, unmistakably, was Lucy W. Weir. I gasped.

"How did this get in there?" I asked.

"It was over there with the others," he said innocently.

"I'm very sorry," I said, shaking my head, "but this book isn't for sale. It's from my private collection. My assistant must have found it behind the counter and put it out by mistake." Since I had no assistant in sight, and my voice was quivering a little, it must have sounded like an outright lie. But he didn't argue. He was probably in a hurry to be on his way before the storm got its second wind.

"Fine," he said, picking up the others and thanking me again for the umbrella. "If you come across another copy, perhaps you could let me know." He dropped an ordinary-looking business card onto the counter and left quickly.

I opened up the book again. How had I missed it? I knew all the inventory inside out. Had it always been there, or had it been plopped into place during the storm?

I closed it abruptly, with a shiver, and packed it into my knapsack to take home.

◆

The box of Lucy's papers had been standing in my apartment unattended to, just as I'd left it weeks before. With Margielove's death and cremation and all the legal work that had followed, I had almost forgotten it. I wondered if *Central Park* was Lucy's way of making me remember.

I read *Central Park* almost in one sitting. It had been published in 1918. The story was very lightweight, a traditional "women's story" about a romance between a college professor and his female student. I wondered what had happened between 1918 and 1920, when *The Intrepid Ones*, a much more woman-identified story, was published. I thought it must have been Harriet that had happened. The earlier book was dedicated to no one, while *The Intrepid Ones* contained a touching dedication to "Harriet, who knows the reason."

I must admit, I skimmed quite a few pages. *Central Park* did not hold my interest as the other novel had. I put it on the shelf with my lesbian books and expected to hear no more from it. But it had an irritating and otherworldly manner of falling off the shelf. When I had replaced it for the third time, I said out loud, in exasperation, "All right, all right, what *is* it you're trying to tell me?"

I realized, in the stillness that followed my question, that each time it fell the book had splayed open to the final chapter. It was a sentimental ending where the professor and the girl abruptly pick up and get married and honeymoon in Saratoga. Over dinner, as husband and wife, he gives her a brooch and she gives him a beautiful and expensive Italian pen that belonged to her father.

"Write me something beautiful with it," she whispers. And the novel ends with a smile and a squeezing of hands.

"I don't get it," I said, once more aloud, and once more, only silence followed. Soon after, I decided the time had come to explore the box.

◆ 12 ◆

The problem was, I had no time to myself anymore. My time belonged to Out of Time. I worked from ten to seven everyday. It took another hour after closing to clean up and balance the register. I could keep up with the bookkeeping when sales were slow, so evenings were theoretically my own. But I was always so exhausted from working sixty-hour weeks that I couldn't do much but drag home some takeout food and prop myself up in front of the TV. Sometimes Catherine would be waiting for me, but more often not. We saw each other mostly on Sundays, when she volunteered to come by and help in the store. Any spare time I found I spent buying new old merchandise for the store and rooting through antiques catalogues trying to price it.

It became apparent to me why Margielove had had to hire an assistant. And one day, on a particularly hectic Saturday just when Indian summer was upon us and the tourists were flooding the streets, forcing New Yorkers to the country or to their apartments to dig out the air conditioners they had prematurely packed away, I placed an urgent sign in the window for part-time help.

The applicants were a varied bunch. The first was a teenaged boy who communicated mostly in grunts and who cased the joint as I talked. The second was a college girl whose ragged giggle was enough to make me say, "I'm sorry, I'm looking for someone with more experience." There was a Latina who spoke no English. Since I spoke no Spanish, I used sign language and a map, and sent her around the corner to Amsterdam Avenue to a bodega that I knew needed help. Finally, there was an older woman, a retired salesclerk from Macy's, who was looking for a job to supplement her fixed income. She seemed perfect, except that her short-term memory was failing. This seemed like a handicap for a salesperson. I had visions of her forgetting the price of something right after she looked at it and charging too little. It was funny that I expected her to err in that way, not to charge too much. She said she compensated for the faltering memory by writing everything down, which explained why, as we talked, she jotted notes into a small notebook.

"I go through one of these a week," she confided, "and I save them all. I have a complete filing system for them. It's my memory, you see. If I didn't keep them, I'd be lost."

And so I hired her on the spot. I liked her organization, I liked her meticulous handwriting in little spiral notebooks from Woolworth's, I liked the way her eyes sparkled when she told me about her experience. Her name was Frances Posner, but everyone, she said, called her Tuttie. I was sure that Margielove would have hired her, too.

◆

I liked Tuttie's directness. It was so different from my own style. The second day we worked in the shop, she asked me, out of nowhere, "So, sweetheart, are you married?" She had a way, I picked up quickly, of prefacing all her questions with "So."

"No," I said with a little smile. She was a chatty person, and her banter helped the slow hours go much more quickly.

"Never been?" she asked.

"No," I repeated, suddenly realizing it didn't matter if she knew I was a lesbian, since I was the boss.

"Me neither," she said, adding immediately, "but not because I didn't have the offers. There was Martin Rankin and Jules, what was his name, Abramowitz, back in the thirties, just for a start, and a few others I've forgotten. Oh, and you probably won't believe this, but old Mr. Dubinsky upstairs from me just last year! Can you imagine!"

"So why didn't you accept?" I asked, amused and charmed. I had already acquired her speaking habits, after two days.

"Oh, he's eighty-five if he's a day," she said, shaking her head. "Now what would I do with an old fart like that?" She winked at me, her whole face wrinkling up in pleasure. She had to be at least seventy-five.

"And when you were younger?"

"No interest," she said, shrugging her shoulders. "I could never see the sense in it. I liked working, I liked my freedom. I didn't want a husband to wait on and a baby every year. But I was no saint, believe me," she winked again. "You know what I'm talking about, darling?"

"Sure," I grinned.

"And you," she continued, "a gorgeous girl like you, you must have had lots of offers in your day."

She took me by surprise. I had to admit I was thirty-two and had never had a marriage offer from a man, though I'd had one once from a woman, Josie Rabinack, whom I'd dated for about a month in San Francisco, years before I met Catherine. She was fifteen years older than I, much better established, and something of a butch. One night, in the women's bar Maude's, just as I was working up the courage to tell her we were history, she got down on one knee in front of everyone and asked me to marry her.

"We're lesbians," I reminded her. "That's impossible."

"I know a minister who does a service for gay people," she said earnestly, pulling something out of her pocket. To my embarrassment it was a box with a brilliant amethyst ring inside.

"Josie," I said, unkindly pushing the box away, "you hardly know me."

"But I know I want you," she persisted.

After several minutes of back and forth that got us nowhere, I left her still on one knee and beat a retreat from the bar. I thought she was the type who might follow me or harass me with phone calls, but she wasn't. My hope is that she met someone else that night at the bar, took her home, and had the amethyst ring adjusted for her shortly thereafter.

"Well," I answered Tuttie, "just one actually." And then, when that didn't seem to be enough of an answer, I added quickly, "I'm a lesbian."

"Oh," she said, as if I'd said nothing more than the time of day. "Honey, you'll have to tell me what that's like. You know, sometimes I see young girls on the street, about your age, holding hands, and I wonder why that never occurred to me." She broke off with a shrug. "Who can say? So," she grinned as a customer walked in, "you'll have to tell me all about it sometime."

I smiled and admired her as she adeptly engaged the customer in conversation. Within minutes she knew his whole life story and had sold him a couple of carpenter's planes as well.

♦

In a few weeks time Tuttie was ready to solo in the shop. I knew this because I watched her closely for signs of confusion or panic when her memory failed her. But she'd trained herself so well with the notebooks that she never skipped a beat. She always explained the notebook to the customers so they wouldn't get the wrong idea when they found a short white-haired woman following them around jotting down notes.

"Relax, darling, I'm not with the CIA, I'm just getting old," she smiled, and held out her notebook in case there were any doubts. People in New York are more suspicious than people in other places. But customers liked her. She was a natural at sales, which was why she'd spent thirty years behind the jewelry counter at Macy's. "Oh, sweetheart, that's such a gorgeous piece! You have such good taste. That one's my personal favorite," she'd say of practically every item in the shop. But she said it with a slight, feathery touch of the hand and an honest look that meant she believed it. To her, the entire store was gorgeous.

I loved her stories about selling. She worked at Gimbel's

during World War II, behind the candy counter. "Honey, I got to know right away who had money to spend and who was all show. The rich ones from the Upper East Side, they'd come in loaded down with furs and jewels and they'd buy fifty cents worth of chocolate-covered cherries and say 'Charge it!' Then they'd want you to put it in a box and wrap it to boot! Then these old ladies, these old babushkas would come in and buy five, ten dollars' worth of candy for their grandsons overseas. And pay cash. They looked like they had *bupkus*. And they probably did. They probably just had that ten dollars to spend. So after that, lambchop, I learned you don't rush to the rich ladies, like some salesgirls do, you treat everybody just the same."

She was no nonsense with me, always.

"Sweetheart," Tuttie said to me one day, "you spend too much time here. And now with me around you don't need to. Go home, why don't you? So why don't you give that gorgeous girlfriend of yours a call?"

So I did.

◆

"Catherine," I said. We were lying in bed, naked, the bedspread crumpled into a heap at our feet, the sheets moist from our having just had sex. "What do you think will happen to us?"

I did not have to explain what I meant. "If I were a gambler," she said, "I wouldn't bet on our relationship."

I laughed, even though it was deadly serious. "No," I agreed, "neither would I." I turned toward her and propped myself up on one elbow. "Are you interested in anyone else?"

"No," she said. "Though maybe I should be. How about you?"

"Sometimes it feels like I'm involved with Lucy and Harriet," I said hesitantly.

"Well, you are, in a sense," she agreed, sitting up. "I mean, to the point of believing you can talk to them. That's been the root of all our problems, hasn't it?"

That was not exactly true, and I was surprised that she put it so simply. We had had terrible fights about our housing situation before I ever found the scrapbook, neither of us willing to make a sacrifice for the other or find a compromise. We'd had disagreements based on our class backgrounds. I'd felt intellectually unequal and inferior to Catherine. And what had been happening between us lately clearly pointed out the differences in the way we viewed the world. Catherine, the pragmatist, had a rough time with my acceptance of the strange and unnatural. And I often had to stop myself from screaming at her to lighten up.

"Yes," I lied, and it started all over again. I had not lied to her since I came back from my trip upstate.

"Why don't we have a trial separation?" she suggested. "Just till you work these women out of your system."

"Do you think I will?"

She drew a deep, sensual breath in the dark. "No, I'm not sure you will."

I pushed her gently down onto the wet spot of the sheets, wondering if it was the last time I would ever do that.

◆ 13 ◆

Bunches of letters, tied with ribbon. Some Moroccan leather notebooks, well worn. Large brown packages neatly wrapped. All precisely packed away. For history.

The dust made me sneeze repeatedly and uncontrollably. It got into my nose and coated my fingertips with a fine layer of grey. I pulled everything out of Lucy's box and sat with it strewn in a circle around me on my living room floor.

It was all so neatly preserved, so carefully packaged, it was hard to imagine upsetting the order of it. The night before, lying in bed with Catherine, I was just about convinced that I should pack it all up without disturbing it, send it off to Barnard's library with my regards, and get on with my life. But as I was making that decision, I heard a familiar voice speaking familiar words.

"Silly girl," Harriet said to me for the second time, "we found *you.*"

And so the next day, resigned to my fate, I let Tuttie run the shop, coming in only briefly in the morning to reassure myself of what I already knew of her capability. Then I went home and after several cups of coffee, which I drank while circling the box cautiously and with trepidation, I sat down and began emptying it, one piece of Lucy at a time.

Bunches of letters, tied up with ribbon.

They had a sweet, musty smell, as if they'd been scented at one time but only the ghost of a fragrance remained. This may have been just a romantic notion on my part, since the return address clearly said "Miss Harriet Timberlake," and I fully expected that someone like Harriet, whom I knew to be a seductress, would have spritzed her letters with her favorite cologne.

The return address also said "Union Avenue, Saratoga Springs, New York," and I was a bit surprised. I had assumed that when Harriet performed outside of New York, Lucy accompanied her. Then the most surprising thing was the postmark of 1917.

I felt several pairs of eyes on me as I slid the linen sheets from the envelope. They rustled under my touch. I thought I heard someone draw in a deep breath, but it is quite likely that that was me.

September 1, 1917

My dear Miss Weir,

This salutation seems much too formal to me, it seems I know you much better than I do. Can it be that we have only spoken once at length, or have I known you in some other world? I am not a superstitious person or one who believes in other lives, but when I saw you first at my photoplay, it was as if I recognized you at once. Your glance had such a calming effect on me. I had been nervous and giddy to that point, but I suddenly had the strength to do what had to be done.

Did you feel this way, too, that we knew each other at another time?

I know I was miserably shy at dinner, but you are so strong and intelligent that I did not want to speak and have you think me stupid. For I am a silly girl of nineteen, who knows nothing of the world compared to someone of your stature and position.

Yet I felt your interest in me, I felt sure at dinner that you did indeed want to be friends with me. It is only now, at some time and distance from you, that my confidence has waned.

May I hope to be your friend?

If you do not reply to this letter, I will understand. I may have misunderstood your attentions. I know you are very busy with your teaching and writing. I cannot wait to read your novel. I will be the first person in Saratoga to purchase a copy.

I expect to make a trip to New York City in the next month with my mother to inquire after some acting lessons with Mrs. Theodora Winkler, a highly regarded teacher. It would please me greatly to see you then for lunch or supper, or perhaps just for coffee. We will be staying with my mother's sister, Mrs. Elizabeth McClelland, who lives on East 20th Street.

May I hope to see you then?

Wishing you all the best in your many endeavors.

Cordially,

Harriet Timberlake

I lowered the letter slowly into my lap. It was difficult to recognize such a young Harriet. The schoolgirl with a crush on Lucy and a lack of confidence did not match the Harriet who had seduced me in the hotel in Saratoga. What a difference a few years could make.

"Surprised?" Harriet said.

"Well, yes, I guess a little," I said aloud, even though she was only thin air.

I carefully withdrew the next letter from its envelope. It was similar to the first in its tone. Harriet went on for two pages thanking Lucy for answering her first letter. At the end her voice dropped to a confidential whisper.

"I was pleased to see," she wrote, "that you recognized the pen. I will use it now always when I write."

They made a date to meet in New York for lunch. My imagination raced, trying to fill in the details of Lucy's letter and anticipating what that luncheon must have been like. Did they rub knees under the table? Stare at each other longingly? Suddenly, I felt cheated. I wanted to be with them during lunch. I willed myself there, but it didn't work. I didn't know where it had taken place and couldn't picture the setting.

Even ghosts, I suppose, have to have some privacy.

◆

That night, before I went to bed, I did two things. I called Catherine, and I looked through the scrapbook for the first time in weeks.

The call to Catherine went like this.

"Catherine?" I always said it as a question, even though I knew her instantly by her hello.

"Hi there," she said, also a routine of hers.

"What do you think is happening to me?" This was not a usual question.

"I don't know," she faltered.

"Do you think it's crazy to believe in ghosts and things like that?" This was another unusual question. "I mean, really crazy?"

"I don't know," she said again, and there was a long pause. "I guess in certain cultures." It was unlike her not to have a more elaborate opinion.

My stomach turned over suddenly. "Is this a bad time for you?"

"Sort of," she hesitated, a nervous quiver to her voice. "A friend came over for dinner and we were just talking. Can I call you tomorrow?"

Tomorrow, she said, not later. The difference was not lost on me.

"Anyone I know?" I asked, ignoring her question.

"No," she said firmly. "Listen, we may be up late talking. I'll call you tomorrow. Okay?"

Now my imagination was working overtime. I knew all her friends—why didn't she mention a name? Catherine hadn't wasted any time finding another love interest. It hadn't even been twenty-four hours.

So I did the only thing I could. I pulled out the scrapbook, leafing through the pictures till I came to the most haunting one of Harriet, the one that had first caught my attention in the antiques shop.

"Harriet," I said, "do you believe in ghosts?"

She waited till the morning to come to me. I was gently

rustled out of sleep by a warm body crawling under the sheets with me, by a soft mouth pressed to my own, slightly tremoring at my touch. I was fully awake when her hand coaxed my willing thighs apart and pushed several long, graceful fingers inside me. I was not startled in the least. I had, in a way, requested it.

And when I came, loudly and resoundingly, it was the single word "Harriet" that left my lips.

♦

Of course, ghosts don't stick around for coffee and bagels. They are part of a different dimension. If they eat and drink at all, it is not because they have to. When my alarm woke me late that morning, I was alone, with a headache, lying in a wet spot on the sheets.

I immediately went to the living room. The box was as I left it, with the contents spilled out on the floor around it. At first glance anyway, it did not look like Harriet had "borrowed" anything. But when I peered into the box, I saw something that had not caught my eye before, if in fact it had been there before. It had rolled to the side and rested there in the shadows. Only a glint from the overhead light made it catch my eye.

It was an exquisite black and gold fountain pen.

I lifted it carefully from the box and ran my fingers over it appreciatively, as I had that morning over Harriet's cool skin. They had an amazingly similar feel.

Was this the pen Harriet had written about in the letter? The more I touched it, the surer I felt.

But the voice I heard then, surprisingly, was not Harriet's. It was deeper, older, Lucy in her prime. "Write me something beautiful with it," she said, quoting her own book. Or had her book imitated life?

I could think of nothing to say but "I will."

♦ 14 ♦

Now that I had a business, with an employee, I was no longer the carefree graduate school dropout. I opened the store at ten, as I always did, and worked a slow morning till Tuttie arrived at noon. I studied the inventory and realized I would have to go on a buying trip soon or resort to the unethical tactics of some other antiques store owners. There was a network of shopkeepers who sold antiques only because there was a market for them, and who tomorrow might be opening a chocolate chip cookie franchise, if that seemed more lucrative. They preyed on older people, women mostly, by visiting the recently widowed or those whose families were packing them off to nursing homes on Long Island. Valuable antiques could be had for a song that way. Margielove had told me a horror story of a shop owner who bragged he had gotten a Tiffany lamp from a woman for two hundred dollars, then turned around and resold it for twenty times that much. The older women had then introduced him to some of her friends. And so on. Sometimes I wondered if the whole antiques business wasn't unscrupulous. It was not much better for me to travel upstate, buy things from country folk, and bring them back to mark up for the yuppies.

Tuttie arrived with her lunch sack, a worn brown bag she carried every day and folded up to take home at night.

"They don't give these out much anymore," she told me the first day. "Everything's plastic now. So I save 'em." I had switched to plastic bags at the store, too, so I was a little embarrassed. Her lunch, as always, was homemade tuna salad on

90

white bread with an apple. She ate it when things were slow. Sometimes it took her hours to finish; sometimes, like today, she ate it all in one sitting.

"Tuttie," I said, "I'm going to have to go away soon, on a buying trip. Will you be able to work full time? It'll be just a few days."

"Sure, hon," she said, cheerfully. She had already told me I was the best boss she had ever had, not like the stuckup young buyers at Macy's. "Where are you going?"

"Probably upstate."

"Oh, that's nice. I went upstate a couple of times when I was younger. I liked that resort, what's it called, Lake George. You probably didn't guess this, but I was a pretty good swimmer."

"No," I smiled, "I didn't." It was hard to imagine Tuttie in a bathing suit.

"That's how I kept my girlish figure," she chuckled, smoothing her skirt across her flat stomach and hips. It was quite a sexy movement. Blushing a little, I turned away and started paying some bills.

But Tuttie, as always, kept talking. "So how's that gorgeous girlfriend of yours? What's her name again?"

"Catherine Synge. We had nice time the other night," I admitted but blushed again, uncontrollably, at the memory of this morning with Harriet. "But things between us aren't that good. I think we're going to separate for a while."

"Sex problems?" she asked bluntly, taking a crisp bite from her apple.

"No," I said, "never that. It's other things."

"Different backgrounds maybe?" she asked.

When we were first together, we'd had problems stemming from my ignorance of the world in which Catherine had grown up, where concern about money and the lack of it played a big part. But that was not really our problem.

"No," I said, dismissively, "that's not exactly it."

Tuttie didn't pry further, though she probably would have liked to. My tone clearly said we should drop it.

"I'm sorry to hear that, sweetheart," she said, with genuine sympathy. "You make a gorgeous couple."

While she chomped her apple, I asked, suddenly, "Tuttie, do you believe in ghosts?"

"So what brings that up?"

"Just making conversation," I said. In my mind, the question followed from the mention of Catherine, but Tuttie could not have understood how.

She swallowed a bite of apple and put the half-eaten, browning core down behind the counter. She was thinking it over very seriously, trying to remember if she had an opinion on the topic.

"There was my aunt Esther, of course," she said. "She died tragically, when she was a young girl, about twenty or so. I don't remember exactly. She never got married or moved from my grandmother's house. She drowned in a rowboat accident in Central Park. Hard to believe, huh? People said it was no accident. She was with her jealous sister Rachel at the time. The story was that they were both in love with the same man, but he wanted Esther. Then there was this mysterious accident with Rachel on the lake in Central Park. Rachel survived, but poor Esther went under. And then Rachel married the man." Tuttie shook her head sadly. "After that, people in my grandmother's house claimed Esther's ghost was there. They actually heard her crying 'Why? Why? Why?' and 'Harold.' That was the boyfriend's name. My uncle Mordecai used to say he saw her, too, but he was just a kid then, and you know what imaginations kids have."

"I know a lot of people who claim to have seen ghosts," I said. "That story of yours sounds like ones I've heard in other families. You know, about the relative who came to a bad end or left something unfinished and now roams around, dissatisfied, as a ghost. I remember my mother was terrified when she buried her mother that if the funeral wasn't according to Grandma's wishes, she'd come back to haunt her."

Tuttie had resumed eating her apple. "I don't know what I think, lambchop. But then I've never seen a ghost myself."

"Yes," I said, "I guess that makes a difference."

The words I'd spoken to Tuttie kept echoing in my mind. "Someone who comes to a bad end or who's left something unfinished." I had often wondered why Sarah Stern and Elinor Devere had left me alone. At first I thought the pull to Lucy and Harriet was stronger because it was Lucy's scrapbook I found. Sarah and Elinor looked attractive enough from the pages of the album, but I reasoned that they just hadn't caught my fancy, that there was no chemistry between us. But as I became more deeply involved with Lucy and Harriet, I wondered if it were not something more profound than that.

I looked up Sarah Stern's dates again, the ones Roz at the Archives had dragged out when Catherine and I visited. 1890-1964. She probably died of some normal disease of old age. Seventy-four was a respectable number of years to live. I had nothing about Elinor, but I was developing a shaky theory anyway. What if they'd lived to ripe old ages, and Lucy and Harriet had not? Letty King had told me that Lucy had a breakdown when Letty "was a girl," after Harriet... died. Well, it was still difficult to think about the two of them in terms of death. I liked the ambiguity surrounding the end of Lucy's life—1890-? A bit like King Arthur, maybe she just went off quietly somewhere and was destined to return at the proper time.

As for Harriet, I had romantic images of her dying tragically, maybe even violently, at a young age. Never becoming a great actress, maybe never even getting to Broadway.

The questions began to mount up. And for some reason, I thought the answers would be clearer if I got out of the city.

◆

The day I was packing for my short trip upstate, a package arrived in the mail. I recognized its source immediately. It had the same heavy brown paper, the same sealing with waterproof tape, and the same method of address as the first package I had gotten like it. It was a flat parcel with considerable padding, marked FRAGILE right next to my name. Inside, beautifully framed in elegant, hand-tooled leather was a portrait of Lucy Warner Weir, from the shoulders up.

It was a hand-colored sepia, the kind my mother had told me was popular when she was young. An artist had actually painted the photograph, adding a blush to the cheeks and a hint of blue to the eyes. The whole effect was soft, hazy, glowing, and a bit haunting. By Lucy's flat, broad-brimmed hat, I guessed the photo was taken later than the twenties. Under the hat showed the edges of a marcel hairstyle. Catherine could have told me which year exactly, but I suspected it was the thirties. Lucy's face, too, looked older, more careworn, accented at the eyes with a web of character lines. The photo showed the top of her dark grey suit, with a silky white blouse fastened at the neck with a pin. The pin was distinctive, a long, sleek onyx and marcasite one that resembled a man's tie clip. The style was enjoying a revival. The framing of the photo was obviously original. A tattered and yellowed label on the back read, "L. B. Andrews & Sons, London."

With the photo, as with *The Intrepid Ones*, came a note on elegant linen stationery, not dissimilar to the kind Harriet had used to write to Lucy.

My dear Miss Van Dine,
    With my compliments. It is about time we met again.
                                                    Best regards,
                                                    Beatrice Best

But there was no phone number or return address, and the phone book listed only B. Best's who weren't the one I wanted. I spoke to an annoyed Benjamin, Barney, and Bertha before giving up the search in that manner.

She didn't want me to find her, I concluded. Like everyone else involved in this game, she would find me when the time was right. After all, she said only that it was "about time." I put the photograph in my bedroom, on the dresser, and finished packing for Saratoga.

◆

On my way out of town, I stopped off at Out of Time to check on Tuttie. There was really no reason to check on her, but it was the first time I'd left the store for more than a day. She was finishing her tuna salad sandwich when I arrived.

"Hi, boss," she said with a smile. "Wanna bite?"

"No thanks," I said.

"Then can I interest you in some tuna salad?" she giggled, and I smiled. She had trapped me in bad vaudevillian jokes before.

"Very funny," I laughed. "But seriously folks. . ." I noticed a wad of tissue paper on the counter and started to crumple it up to throw away, when a pinpoint inside the wrapper pricked me. "Ouch," I moaned, leaving a dot of bright red blood on the paper.

"Uh-oh," Tuttie said, jumping up and wiping her hands on her skirt before touching the paper. "Careful, sweetheart. There's something gorgeous inside. My first purchase for the store." She looked suddenly embarrassed. "I hope it's okay, hon. I wouldn't have done it but believe me, baby, I know jewelry and this was a buy."

She carefully unfolded the paper to reveal a long, sleek onyx and marcasite pin, a carbon copy of the one in Lucy's portrait.

"Where'd you get this?" I practically shouted.

"A gal brought it in here, looking to sell," Tuttie explained. "Only wanted ten dollars for it. Can't figure it. She was a dealer, too. You can easily sell it for fifty, maybe even seventy-five. My mother gave me a pin like this when I got my first job, at a dress shop downtown. Girls are wearing them again." She was holding it delicately, so I could see the workmanship. "Nice, huh, lambchop?"

I nodded weakly. I held onto the counter for support. "Who," I began shakily, "who was this 'gal' you bought it from?"

"Oh," she hesitated, not sure of her memory, "an older girl, not as ancient as me, not as young as you. A ladylike little thing. Dark suit, I think, looked hot as hell. Hair done up in a bun. Yes, a bun. Kind of salt-and-pepper hair."

"She didn't leave her name?" I ventured.

"As a matter of fact," Tuttie said, first consulting her notebook, then reaching under the counter to a box where we kept customers' business cards, "she did." She held it out to me, and I took it with trembling fingers. "Hey, cupcake, you better sit down, you look all white... like you've seen a ghost," she chuckled.

The card read, "The Best Years of Our Lives, Antiques and Collectibles," with the address. Underneath, it said, "Beatrice Best, Proprietor."

◆ 15 ◆

Needless to say, I postponed my trip. I felt I had been summoned. It was funny, but seeing the shop again, facing my crime, possibly having to return the scrapbook did not frighten me as it once had. Beatrice Best, who sent presents in the mail and sold my clerk merchandise for way below its value, suddenly felt like a friendly figure.

I went the next day, and appropriately, it was raining. The scene felt decidedly like a case of déjà vu, except that this time I carefully noted the sign above the door, a hand-painted one with the words written in an elegant script. I had to tilt my umbrella to look at it, and it occurred to me that was why I hadn't noticed it the first time.

The interior had changed only slightly—the settee had not been sold, but the clothing on it had changed to a beaded flapper's dress with a feather boa. The bell tinkled in just the same way as before, but Bea Best was different than I remembered. There was more grey in her hair, her frame was slighter, her fingers looked less nimble. It took her longer to come from the back room. When she smiled, it almost seemed to hurt her.

"Oh," she said, without greeting, "I see it's still pouring." She came right out into the middle of the store and took my hand. "Let's go into the back," she said simply.

The back room was a combination office and storage room. The walls were lined with dark bookcases, and there was a humpback sofa that matched the settee in the outer room. A beautiful oak roll-top desk held a prominent place

97

against the nearest wall. Above it hung an oil painting of someone who looked amazingly like Lucy Warner Weir, but was not her. The room, unlike the back rooms of many shops, was neat and attractive enough to have been the actual sales area.

A lamp on the portrait was one of the few lights in the room. We sat on the sofa in shadows, behind a table where coffee for two had been arranged. It was hot, as if Beatrice had been expecting me.

"The woman in the portrait was my mother," Bea explained, though I hadn't asked. "That was painted in 1923, before I was born. In fact, she was probably pregnant with me at the time she sat for it."

"She was lovely," I said, a strange choice of words for me, a phrase I'd rarely used before. The ambience seemed to call for it.

"She looks a lot like Aunt Lucy," she noted further. "Especially around the eyes. But the mouth is different. Mother's thin lips were the bane of her existence."

I nodded and drank my coffee, the cup making a tiny tinkle in the silence as I brought it down to the saucer.

Suddenly, she said, "Why did you come?"

I swallowed hard and looked startled. She had caught me completely offguard. "Well," I said, "it seemed to be more your idea than mine."

"Yes," she agreed, "that's true. But why did you come?" she repeated as if this were a test and I'd given the wrong answer.

"To thank you?" I asked. "For, you know, the book and the photo and the pin."

"You're welcome," she said. "But you could have done that in a note. I did leave you my address."

"Yes," I faltered.

"So, Miss Van Dine, why are you here?" she persisted, a look of intensity on her face.

I deflected the question, composing myself and trying to take control. "If I tell you the truth, will you answer some questions for me?"

"It depends," she said, looking off into the other room as the front door bell rang. "Excuse me," she said, getting up.

I could hear her voice and that of a customer muffled through the damask curtain. There was a lengthy exchange, the bell tinkled again, and she had returned within a few minutes.

"Sixties memorabilia," she said with a disapproving nod. "I won't carry it. I won't pander to such tastes." She sat on the sofa again, at the far end from me.

"What is it you want to know?" she asked.

"Why you sent the presents," I said quickly, "and how you knew Out of Time was my store."

"It's a small world of antique dealers," she explained, ignoring the first question. "Word gets around. I heard about Marjorie's tragic death. And though your store is hardly an antiques shop," she said with a disdainful look, "we are sort of in the same business. I must say you've improved the quality of merchandise tremendously."

"And the presents," I continued, suddenly disappointed that she hadn't just known telepathically. "Why did you send them, after I took your scrapbook?"

"The more interesting question, don't you think, is why did you take the scrapbook?" She peered at me over her cup. "And why are you here now?"

"How did you know I'd come today, just now?"

"A hunch," she said, smiling vaguely.

There was a long silence, during which she sipped her coffee and offered me some oatmeal cookies. She was not about to ask her question again, but something made me answer it anyway.

"I came because Lucy Weir and Harriet Timberlake are haunting me," I blurted out, fully aware of how ludicrous it must have sounded. I suddenly remembered I was a rational thinker, a woman with advanced degrees, at least one of which, the M.B.A., should exclude me from a belief in ghosts. But Beatrice didn't look startled in the least. She set her cup down carefully and wordlessly.

"They've haunted me from the first day in this shop," I

continued, a panic in my voice. "They pop out of pictures, they talk to me, they send me postcards. I don't know what to do."

"Does it frighten you?" she asked.

"No," I said, after a moment's thought. "Not really."

"Do they do you harm?"

"Of course not," I laughed.

"And would you like them to stop?"

I hesitated again, thinking of how my life had changed since that first rainy afternoon. Aside from the separation from Catherine, my life had become fuller and taken on more meaning. Parts of it were almost exciting. "No," I answered.

She brushed some cookie crumbs from her skirt. "Then what do you want?" she asked, more with concern than irritation.

"I want to know why," I said. "Why me. What they want. Where this will lead. What I'm to do. If I'm some special person picked out by them for something, I have to know why."

"That's a big bill," she said. The bell in the front room sounded again. This time she was gone for ten minutes or more. I got up, stretched, perused the bookshelves, fingered a few papers on her desk. On it was a copy of *Photoplay* magazine from 1927. As I was picking it up, she reentered the room.

"Take it," she said, as I was dropping it back to the desk. "It may help."

I was about to say "With what?" when she got my umbrella from the corner and handed it to me. "It's stopped raining," she said. "I have to spend some time with these particular customers. But please feel free to come again. I'll think about your questions."

But I had another confession to make, and it couldn't wait. "Your aunt's papers, her journals and such..."

"I don't have them," she frowned, in a hurry to get rid of me.

"I know. I do."

I guess nothing much surprised Bea Best. "And how did you do that?"

"I bought them from your sister," I answered. "I didn't

know then how to reach you. If you want them..."

She glanced anxiously towards the shop. "They belong with the scrapbook," she snapped. "And we both know who has that."

She held the damask curtain open for me. In the front room a man and woman were inspecting jewelry in the case. They smiled at me as I passed behind the counter. Outside the air after the rain was thick and muggy. The thought of riding the subway in the heat made me feel claustrophobic. As on that first afternoon, I took a cab uptown.

◆

I was very confused. I replayed the scene in the shop over in my mind as I stood amid the historic debris in my living room. Although Beatrice had seemingly summoned me, had expected me, she had nothing really to tell me and even looked a little put out by my presence. She dismissed me as casually as she might have brushed some dust from her merchandise.

I had expected something different, some startling revelations, or some help in figuring out what I had become a part of. Instead, she was as controlling and evasive as Harriet. It was clear that I'd been given only a puzzle, in a thousand pieces, without the accompanying picture to show what the finished product looked like. With my time as minimal as it was, I could continue to piece it together for years without knowing exactly what I was doing.

I sat down heavily on the sofa. I could not open the scrapbook on the table. I couldn't stand to see the beckoning eyes, the almost taunting smiles. Why me? What did they want of me? If I chose, couldn't I just walk away from the whole thing—pack up all my material on Lucy and Harriet and send it downtown to Bea? This had crossed my mind more than once. In fact, in mentioning the box to Bea, I had half hoped she would request that.

I picked up the phone and dialed Catherine's number. We were supposed to call less, under our new arrangement, but I hadn't been good at honoring that.

"Hi. This is Catherine's answering machine. Catherine can't come to the phone right now. Please leave a message for her after the beep."

I sat with the phone to my ear, listening to the long beep and the stillness that followed. I breathed softly into the phone, picturing Catherine out on a date, or worse yet, in the middle of sex. Too much soft breathing had gone by, and now I was too embarrassed to admit who it was. I hung up quietly.

Then I suddenly remembered my bag. I'd stuffed the old *Photoplay* into it without looking at it. It couldn't hurt to see what was in it. Maybe Bea had put it out on purpose, to give me the key to the whole mystery. Or maybe if it wasn't exactly a pass-key to all the closed doors in front of Lucy and Harriet, it would be like a file to pick the locks with.

I read it cover to cover. The truth is, I kind of enjoyed it. I'd spent so much time being a serious student of literature that I'd missed the things popular culture is made of—things like *Photoplay*, *True Confessions*, *Modern Romance*. I read or glanced over every bit of it. I found out where, in 1927, you might send for a pattern to make a dress like the one Louise Brooks wore in *Love 'Em or Leave 'Em*. I read all about "It", a euphemism for sex appeal, and why Clara Bow had so much. Her new movie by that name had just been released. Even the ads used movie stars: "When Constance Bennett dashes out into the pouring rain to keep a location date for *Into the Net* she finds complete protection in the donning of her Radio Oiltex Slicker." And there was a minor article about an innovation that no one believed would amount to much—the introduction of sound to silent films, making them "part-talkies."

As quaint and interesting as it was, there seemed to be nothing pertaining to my particular interest. It was all motion picture gossip, nothing about stage actors and actresses. I briefly considered selling the magazine in the store, but then remembered Bea's "It may help" and thought better of it. What it would help with, if anything, remained to be seen.

♦ 16 ♦

I had every intention of spending a day and a half on the road, mostly in the Woodstock and New Paltz area, looking for bargains for the shop. So the intentions were there. I even spent almost a day doing just that. I hit every junk shop that looked like it was run by a close friend of Margielove's—people for whom time, after the Nixon reelection, was irrelevant. They had lots of interesting things at prices I could afford—stoneware jugs, washing boards, country cookware—all things I knew New York yuppies loved to decorate their apartments with. It was ironic, because these were items the middle class of one hundred years ago would never have owned—they would have considered them too countrified. Now, at a safe distance of time and place, the middle class wanted to recapture the roots it never actually had.

One of the shopkeepers recognized me from Margielove's funeral. He had heard about it through the grapevine and had ventured into New York for the service we held at her apartment. I had assumed by their appearance that most of the people at the service were street people, but it turned out this was incorrect.

"You're the one she left everything to," he said, remembering the events of the day. I was suddenly afraid, alone in an old barn with a guy who had not shaved or had his hair cut since 1970. There was some innocence in his eyes, though, or maybe it was the glassy look that comes from drugs. It was difficult to distinguish in the dim lighting of the barn.

"Yeah," I said in a low voice, checking over my shoulder

so I knew exactly where the door was.

"Man, you're lucky," he smiled. "She was some rich chick." He looked down at his feet, chuckling to himself. "It's funny, huh? She had this rich old man she didn't want any part of, he was some nuclear physicist or something. She split that whole deal, split the rich bitch college he sent her to. But he left her a lot of bread anyway. What a trip. And now," he laughed, "it goes to her old lady! What a joke on him, huh?"

I started to explain that I wasn't her "old lady," but there seemed to be no point to that. Let the hippies think she'd had the last laugh on her wealthy, establishment father by leaving his money to her lesbian lover. Laughing with him at the irony of it, I bought a few crocks, an old quilt that would need cleaning, and a couple of tin mechanical banks. Out of some duty to Margielove, I left him my card, in case he was ever in New York.

"Hey, thanks, man," he said, but I doubted, by the way he stuffed it into his jeans pocket, that he'd ever find that card again.

♦

I don't know why my car headed for Saratoga, but it did. It was not as if it were a stone's throw away; it was more like a two-hour trip from where I was. It was a decision I made without thinking, almost as if I got on the Thruway heading in the wrong direction and never corrected the situation. I didn't stop till I reached the information booth in downtown Saratoga Springs.

"Do you have a phone book?" I asked. The attendant pulled out a slim volume and I thumbed through it quickly, my finger running down the columns of "T's." Quickly I jotted down a name I found on Union Avenue, thanked the information clerk, and picked up a city map. Then I strolled across the street to the hotel and made a phone call.

♦

Mrs. Roger Timberlake was not that happy to hear from

me, but she agreed to let me stop by her house on Union Avenue. It was an elegant, slim, three-story frame house with delicate gingerbread carving under the cornice. Like many structures in town, it had been built over a hundred years before, during Saratoga's heyday, but had been maintained so well it still looked new.

"Come in," she said, rather crisply, but politely just the same. She was a small, neat woman in her sixties, with dark hair that had just a hint of grey at the temples. Her parlor was impeccably furnished in the Queen Anne style. At the picture window was a baby grand piano, top heavy with family photographs. I did not see any of Harriet.

"What sort of research did you say you are doing?" she asked, with a thin, Nancy Reagan kind of smile.

"On early twentieth-century actresses," I lied, so adept at it by now it came out without a moment of thought or hesitation. "I found a reference to Harriet Timberlake in some newspaper articles I was reading."

"That was my husband's aunt," she said. "I don't know much about her. She was sort of the black sheep of the family. Ran off to New York at nineteen or twenty. *To be with another woman,*" she said, with emphasis, but lowering her voice at the same time. I thought we were alone in the house, but she continued to whisper. "You know what I mean. Broke her mother's heart. She used to come back to Saratoga, sometimes to be in plays, and sometimes just on vacation, and always tried to get back into her family's graces. They never really reconciled. I heard she eventually started seeing men, straightening out a little, but I couldn't swear to it. She was an actress, and who knows what kind of wild things they do?"

Men? I almost choked, but I regained my composure beautifully. "Do you know what happened to her?" I asked.

"She was just a minor actress, I'm surprised you've heard of her. Did summer stock here and other places, a few movies. I can't remember. She never became a star, anyway. I seem to recall she was going to go to Hollywood but something happened. She got killed in an accident when she was still in her twenties."

"Would your husband know more details?" I ventured.

Her face suddenly clouded over. "He would. But my husband died last year." The pain, I could tell by her look, was still close to the surface.

"I'm sorry," I said, then I didn't know what else to say.

She ran a hand over her cheek, smoothing the skin, pushing the tears back in. "He was the last of the Timberlakes up here. Harriet had only one brother, my husband's father. My husband was an only child. We had four girls, all married now."

"I'm sorry," I said again, realizing it sounded like I was sorry they had four girls.

Her face brightened a little. "There was a scrapbook my husband kept when he was a little boy about his aunt. He adored the movies and apparently thought it was romantic to have an aunt who was an actress. She wrote to him, too, but I think his mother eventually got rid of the letters. The scrapbook, though, I've seen that." She looked perplexed. "I'll have to think about where it is. I haven't seen it in a long time."

"If you remember where it is, maybe I could visit again," I said, handing her my card. "I'd love to see it."

She took the card hesitantly, probably not sure she should get involved. "Yes," she said.

I thanked her and left. And then my car started heading south, out of town.

♦

Only a day and a half had passed since I had left but it felt longer, probably because I had packed a lot into such a short time. Driving across the George Washington Bridge, back to Manhattan, down the Henry Hudson Parkway to the Seventy-ninth Street exit, I had a sudden feeling of panic and nausea. I had done this before, come back from a hectic trip to find the shop closed and Margielove dead. I had a clear image of Tuttie, smiling and waving half a tuna sandwich at me as I entered the store, then a sense of dread that I should have never left her alone.

But as I pulled up in front of the store with my heart pounding, the fear subsided. There was Tuttie in the window, with a feather duster in her hand.

"Hi, boss," she said with a big grin. "So how's the North Country?"

"Swell," I said, my vocabulary oddly resembling hers. "So how's the junk business?"

"Darling, it couldn't be better," she said, earnestly. "Yesterday was busy, busy, *busy*." She waved her arms as she spoke, a cloud of dust flying off her feather duster back onto the merchandise. "Thank God you got more stuff," she said, glancing out at the filled station wagon, which I was watching too, for vandals. "I sold those pressed back chairs and the overstuffed chair and the little round mahogany table," she continued, hardly breathing. "So guess how much I got for the table?"

She ran down a short list of other bulky items; in glancing around quickly I noticed a certain emptiness to the room. I was glad I hadn't hesitated over a humpback trunk that was a bit overpriced: it would take up some of the floor space.

"Oh, and lovey, I was right about that onyx pin!" she almost squealed. My heart sank, remembering I hadn't put it away or instructed her not to sell it. "Seventy-five dollars! I'm becoming a real dealer, huh?" She looked so proud of herself, I couldn't tell her. But I felt a little woozy, like I'd come home to find my Lucy Weir collection distributed to the highest bidders.

"That's great," I said weakly. Noticing some young boys eyeing my car, I decided to unpack. "You are quite a saleswoman."

Tuttie and I spent the next couple of hours logging in the new merchandise and pricing it. Then we arranged the larger items in the blank spaces left by Tuttie's phenomenal selling day. We finally finished a little after closing time, and Tuttie, who wasn't used to working full-time, looked haggard. I offered to buy her dinner after we locked up. To my surprise she chose a vegetarian restaurant in the neighborhood, and then picked an avocado and sprout sandwich from the menu and vegetarian chili. I couldn't pass up the opportunity to tease her.

"I don't know, Tuttie," I smiled, "pretty soon you'll be coming to work with crystals around your neck, wearing Birkenstocks."

She looked at me blankly, and I described the kind of sandal I meant.

"Oh," she said, seriously, "those do look kinda comfy."

"Why the sudden craving for vegetables?" I asked.

She looked still more serious, uncharacteristically so. Tuttie without her one-liners was unfamiliar, like waking up unexpectedly in a strange bedroom and not knowing where you are.

"Darling, I eat tuna salad sandwiches everyday because they're cheap," she sighed. "For breakfast, I allow myself one piece of toast, and on the weekends an egg. For dinner, I make a big pot of soup and eat that all week, too. I got it down to a science, how to eat all week on twelve-fifty." She took a big bite of avocado sandwich and chewed slowly, thoughtfully. "You're nice enough to take me out, I want something different, something I wouldn't ever fix at home in a million years."

I felt suddenly stupid and self-centered for not putting two and two together. I thought she just liked tuna sandwiches. I almost said, I wish I had known, I'd have insisted on a nicer place, someplace with a lot of seafood and sun-dried tomatoes. But that would have sounded like charity. Instead, I watched her eat every last bite of her dinner with real appreciation, and I knew that a raise was long overdue.

"Tuttie," I asked, "do you by any chance remember who bought that onyx pin?"

She looked confused and knitted her eyebrows, furiously trying to remember on her own. Then, she pulled out one of her spiral notebooks and flipped through the pages.

"I didn't write down the name," she sighed, but then her

face brightened. "But she paid by check! I remember that! It's not written down here, but I'm sure. Why?"

"Just curious," I said.

"If it's who I think it was, she was an old woman, a little tottery. Older than me, even," she chuckled. "Yes, I remember when she held out her hand for the pin, I noticed how wrinkled it was. She had a younger woman with her, maybe a daughter." She looked worried. "Didn't you want to sell it?"

"Of course I did," I lied. "I was really just curious."

I paid the bill, then drove Tuttie back to her apartment. It was around ten o'clock, and I offered to escort her upstairs but she declined.

"Dinner was swell," she smiled through the open car window. I waited till she was safely inside. Then I drove right back to the store, and got out the deposit envelope, which I kept locked in a drawer overnight till I could get to the bank in the morning. Tuttie had closed out while I finished rearranging the furniture.

There were only a few checks, and the one I wanted but never expected to find was right on top. Clearer than anything, in bold block letters, it said "Elinor Devere" across the top.

◆ 17 ◆

I can't say why I did what I did next. It was as if again my car had a mind of its own, or I had forgotten some very important part of my recent past. Because before I knew it, I had fought the downtown traffic and found myself sitting in the car, right outside of Catherine's apartment, looking up at the third-story front window, where the lights were on in full force. Catherine liked to keep all the lights in the apartment on at once.

When I was sitting there, of course, looking up like that, I realized what a mistake it was. I had been so anxious to tell someone about Elinor, someone who knew the story—and that meant Catherine—that I had raced there without remembering we were separated, that Catherine might even be dating someone else. That was the thought that got me out of the car, to the door, to the intercom, where I pressed the buzzer marked "Synge" with three short beeps.

Through the static came the familiar voice. "Yes?"

"Catherine, it's Susan."

There was a long pause, then she buzzed to let me through the security door. I took the steps to the third floor two at a time.

Before the separation, I had my own key. If I forgot it, Catherine would wait at the door when I buzzed to welcome me with a kiss. I could see her at the turn to the last half-flight of steps.

Tonight she was waiting at the door with a stern look on her face, which erased the smile from mine.

"Susan," she said, "you should have called."

I stopped just short of the last step, my legs poised at two different levels. I could have, if necessary, pivoted 180 degrees and headed back down as quickly as I came.

But I stood my ground.

"You're busy," I said. "I know it's late."

"Yes, I'm busy," she said, guarding the doorway. "You should have called."

"You have company," I said, my heartbeats pounding in my chest.

There was a delicate, smooth intake of breath that meant she was impatient with me and tired of the conversation.

"No," she said, to my surprise, "that's not it."

I took the last few steps and stood in front of her, my head lowered apologetically. "I'm sorry," I said, "I just had something great to tell you."

She moved her hands to the door, getting a firmer grip. She sighed again. "You really should've called. Those are the rules. We're separated. We don't drop in unannounced anymore. That's why we gave back each other's keys."

"But you drop in on friends of yours," I argued, knowing I was going to lose. "You know, like Georgia and Gail."

"That's different," she frowned. "Tell me, if I *had* someone here now, how would you feel?"

I didn't have to think about it very long. "I'd want to kill her," I said, then added quickly, "figuratively speaking."

"Figuratively speaking," she repeated, smiling a little. "Anyway, it's just respectful to call first. And safer," she grinned.

"Now that I'm here," I said, "and you don't have *company*, may I come in?"

The smile flickered and faded. "Let's go out," she said. "I'm a little hungry, and there's a place that's still open."

"You don't trust me?" I said with concern, as she let me in the door for just a minute while she went to get her wallet.

"It isn't that," she insisted. "I said I'm hungry."

What I glimpsed of the apartment looked different, in just

a few weeks time. There were some new prints and a brightly colored throw cover on the old sofa. The living room looked livelier, happier. I didn't say that though.

"You have some new things," is what I said.

She was back with her wallet already. "Yeah, I realized how little I was here when we were together and how dark I'd let it become. It's weird how you let things slide when you're in a couple. I'd really like some new furniture, get away from this Salvation Army decor."

"It looks nice," I said sadly, following her back out the door. She hadn't let me into the bedroom. That, I figured, had really changed, maybe had her new lover's clothes strewn across the floor, a picture of the two of them on the dresser in a romantic embrace. I had to ask.

"And the bedroom? Did you change that, too?" But she was already locking the apartment door behind us.

"What?" She looked more deadpan than puzzled. "Oh, no. No, that's just the same."

She started down the stairs, and I followed.

◆

We went to a place I'd never been to before. Catherine ordered a pork bun and I had some tea because I wasn't hungry but I felt obliged to order something. My elation at finding a check with Elinor's name on it had collapsed sometime during the incident at Catherine's apartment. In fact, I had forgotten why I had come to see her at all, till we faced each other solemnly across the table and Catherine asked.

"Oh, yes," I answered, "I have something great to tell you." All of sudden, seeing her look up at me expectantly, I realized she might not regard the news as great. She saw my obsession with Lucy Weir and her friends as the reason for our separation. I remembered this in an instant, though when I had driven downtown to tell her, I only thought how thrilled as a historian she would be.

"Maybe you won't think it's so great," I backed down.

"Try me," she said through a mouthful of bun.

"Elinor Devere is still alive," I said hurriedly. "You know, one of the women in the scrapbook."

She stopped eating and reached across the table for my hand, in a movement she could not have thought about in advance. Once there, her hand, resting on mine, squeezing it slightly, trembled a little, hesitated, and drew back.

"Susan, that's wonderful," she smiled. "I'm happy for you."

I unraveled the story of the onyx pin for her, right to the part where I'd jumped into my car and headed down to her apartment. She nodded and forgot she was annoyed with me.

"What made you go look for the check?" she asked, resuming her eating.

I hesitated, knowing this brought me even further into the murky waters of spirits, ghosts and intuition. How strange would this whole incident seem to her? How strange did it seem to me?

"I had a feeling," I said, "I can't describe it. Like I knew the pin being bought had some meaning. Like it wasn't just bought by someone casually off the street."

"Wow," Catherine said, thinking that over a moment. "This whole thing is really bizarre. First Beatrice, then Elinor finding your shop. It's hard for me to believe." She finished eating, and reached over to squeeze my hand again. Our ankles grazed under the table. As they did, I was suddenly and uncontrollably wet between the legs.

"It's just great," she continued. "If she'll talk to you, and I don't see why she wouldn't, you can get the whole story. Or one end of it anyway. You won't be so. . . haunted." I inched toward the table, afraid of what came next, the end of our visit, the goodbye at the door of her building. But as we walked back there, bringing each other up to date on our lives in the past weeks, we kept bumping into each other, brushing sleeves and arms, in a way that made the tiny hairs on my arm stand straight up in excitement. By the time we reached the door, we were almost fully leaning into each other in the familiar way of lovers, or the flirtatious way of people who are about to become lovers. At the door, she invited me in, even though it was late and we both had to work the next morning. I went up with her, prepared for rejection and disappointment. But as we entered the apartment, she took my arms firmly and pulled me up against her, so the nipples of our breasts met in welcome. I spent the night, even though nothing made sense and my whole life seemed to consist of a series of accidents and coincidences and unplanned encounters. I spent the night, even though I had no idea what it would be like for us in the morning.

♦

In the morning, Catherine had to go to school, and I had to open the store. I woke up at daybreak on my side facing Catherine, to find her staring at me strangely, like she'd brought someone home from a bar and she didn't know exactly who it was. But we hadn't been drinking at all the night before, and she knew all too well who I was—that was probably why she looked so scared.

"What's wrong?" I said. "How long have you been lying there like that?"

"Nothing's wrong," she said. She sat up and brushed her hair back in way that made me want to see it again on the pillow, fanned out in a soft web. She must have decided instantly to be honest, because she turned back to me with the same look I'd woken up to. "I just wonder what all this means."

It was rhetorical, something she knew I had no better answer for than she did.

She had to crawl over me to the ladder of the loftbed, and just as she was straddling me, I reached for her waist and held her there firmly. Instead of saying "Susan, I have to get up" or "No, not now," she stayed there, sitting on me, her hair falling forward onto my chest. I sat up a little, and took one of her nipples into my mouth. I nibbled at it expertly, just the way she liked, and she moaned softly and threw her hair back so I could glimpse her face. On it were the pain and pleasure that had always gone hand in hand in our relationship. She

114

rubbed back and forth on my stomach until she came, with an enormous cry of relief that must have resounded in several neighboring apartments.

As was her style, she recovered from orgasm almost immediately, not like some lovers who collapse in a heap. Within minutes, she was lying snugly next to me, her hand between my legs, her long, firm fingers pushing into me with her characteristic deftness and skill. I took a long time to come. My mind was racing over all the possibilities of this encounter, what it actually did mean. I didn't relax, didn't let go till she slid down and finished the job with her tongue. I came in a blur of images, thoughts wiped from my mind like chalk by an eraser that leaves a swirl of white behind. Afterwards, we showered separately, left separately, after a tentative but passionate kiss at the front door. I drove uptown in the morning haze, and by the time I got to my apartment, I was wondering if it all had been a dream.

◆ 18 ◆

In my hurry to meet Elinor Devere, I actually considered showing up on her doorstep uninvited. But she had to be at least ninety years old, a ghost from another era, and I decided I should write her a note first. If she didn't respond, I would have to seriously reconsider my strategy.

I planned it all very carefully. I had a print made of one of the photographs in the scrapbook, showing the four of them together in Montauk on a windy bluff. Then I bought some very elegant stationery, the nicest I ever had. In fact, now that I think about it, I'm not sure I ever had stationery before then. I was prone to using the backs of flyers from lesbian events and legal pads I stole from various offices I worked in. The fanciest I'd ever used was the letterhead of Out of Time, that had a cute, folksy logo that hadn't suited Margielove and now didn't suit me. It was a pen drawing of an hourglass resting on a quilt with some other antiques surrounding it. Margielove had obtained it from a five-dollar clip-art book of uncopyrighted designs. The obvious reason they were uncopyrighted was that no one would want to claim such an ugly design.

I couldn't use that to write to Elinor. I had an elegant, creamy linen weave stationery printed with my name and home address. It made me look like someone important, someone people would want to meet, which was the whole idea, since I wanted Elinor to either write back or pick up the phone and call me.

I did several drafts of the letter before committing it to expensive stationery. For the final version, I used the fountain pen I found in Lucy's box, which I refilled and broke in again. It wrote smoothly, like the words were flowing spontaneously out of my fingers to the pen to the paper. "Dear Elinor Devere," it began. (I debated the salutation a long time; I refused to use "Miss," on principle, but surely a ninety-one-year-old woman wouldn't call herself "Ms." Or would she?)

Some time ago I had the good fortune to purchase a scrapbook and photo album containing pictures of yourself, Sarah Stern, Lucy Weir, and Harriet Timberlake. I was so taken by the beauty of the photographs and the warmth in your faces that I have since done some research into the lives of Lucy and Harriet. In a way, I feel haunted by them and must know more. When I saw that you had bought Lucy's onyx pin from my shop, I was thrilled to discover that one of The Gang was still alive, and could, I hope, relate for me what that time and these fascinating people were like.

I included my phone numbers and what I hoped was a sincere plea for her to contact me. Then I enclosed the print and mailed the letter.

The next few days were torture. I was anxious for Elinor to call, and after a week, was convinced that she wouldn't. I had completely abandoned my examination of the contents of Lucy's box, pinning all my hopes on Elinor. Finally, when I couldn't stand the tension any longer, the telephone rang.

◆

Elinor Devere had a companion, someone to answer the phone, read the mail, pay the bills and fix her meals. If Elinor was capable of going to an antiques shop to buy a pin, she was probably capable of doing all those things herself, too. But at that age, who would want to? If I lived as long and hadn't squandered all my money, I hoped to do the same thing.

"This is Emily Fleck, Elinor Devere's secretary," she informed me when she called. She had a crisp British accent and a manner that was cool and off-putting.

"We received your note, but I must tell you that Miss Devere is ninety-one years old. She doesn't give interviews."

"But this is very important," I said. "I'm—I'm writing a book about Lucy Weir, and I need to know everything. Miss Devere's recollections of that time would be so valuable."

There was a long pause. "She's very fit, you know, for ninety-one, but she still tires easily," she said, less haughtily than before. "I really must protect her from over-extending herself."

I requested a series of short sessions, maybe fifteen minutes at most. "I'm sure she'll want to meet me. After all, I have a number of items belonging to Lucy that she might like to see, including some photographs of her and Sarah Stern."

Sarah Stern's name seemed to be the magic word. Fleck made an appointment for me for the following Sunday, at four o'clock. "Her best time, tea time," she explained. "But I'll have to be there also. Just as protection. And at four-fifteen, I'll be escorting you to the door."

Finally, I asked, "Tell me something, if you can. How in the world did you find my shop? How did you know where to find that pin?"

After an uncomfortable silence, Fleck sounded embarrassed by her lack of an answer. "You should ask Miss Devere," she replied, hesitantly. "It was her idea." I opened my mouth to respond, but there was a click on the other end of the line.

◆

When I hung up, I went directly to Lucy's box. I decided to look for anything I could find about Elinor—letters, journal entries. There was, in fact, a packet of letters that were from people other than Harriet. None were from Elinor, but several were from Sarah Stern with postmarks in various locations across France. They were all dated 1917 and 1918. Sarah, it turned out, was driving an ambulance as a volunteer, and had met a number of interesting women, including:

> ... a camp of English girls, members of the V.A.D., daughters of the titled aristocracy. They never lifted a finger for themselves at home, but here they are, mucking about with the rest of us, helping to save lives. Of course, after the war, they'll go back to being waited on hand and foot. But I suppose one must give them a certain measure of credit for coming out here at all.

Later in that letter, Sarah admitted a particular fondness for one of the British ambulance drivers.

> Elinor Devere, her father is Viscount of something or other. Terribly spoiled, but a girl of considerable intellect. We have begun to read together some afternoons between shifts and to discuss what we read in what free time we have. I have only two books with me, *Women and Economics* and *Eighty Years & More*, and she has none, but amazingly is interested in both of those, though I wouldn't describe her as a suffragist. Those times together are the bright spots amid all the horror. I will be sorry to leave this camp, but I follow the American troops. To tell the truth, I am a bit smitten.

There was a last letter from Sarah in England. The armistice had been reached, and she had somehow managed to end up in England, carrying with her the address of Elinor Devere in London. "Well, my friend, when we saw each other again, it was clear what path we would take. We have discussed her coming to New York with me. So maybe I have found my partner now, too, as you have your Harriet!"

There were no more letters from Sarah after that. Presumably, there was no need to write, since Sarah and Lucy both lived in New York City, although at opposite ends of town. I took out the scrapbook and flipped to a snapshot of Sarah and

Elinor at the beach. Sarah, small and feisty, Elinor, large and plump, looking much older than her mid-twenties. I both looked forward to and dreaded my Sunday appointment, when the past would suddenly really come to life.

✦ 19 ✦

Elinor Devere owned a brownstone on Grove Street, the front of which was almost completely obscured by ivy. It was a house I had passed many times and often looked at in admiration, wondering who lived there.

I had put my fears about Catherine taking over my project aside and talked her into coming with me for the meeting. I thought it was important for our relationship. She was hesitant, based on the incident with the Sarah Stern articles. But when it came to talking to Elinor face to face, I was scared, and I admitted it. Catherine had excellent interviewing techniques from years of doing oral histories of immigrants on the Lower East Side. I was afraid I would be too abrupt, too anxious to fit a lot into fifteen minutes, and would alienate Elinor or Emily or both. If that happened, I knew Catherine would take control.

I hadn't asked if I could bring her, though, and Emily Fleck was startled to see both of us at the front door.

"Yes?" she said, as if we might be Jehovah's Witnesses or door-to-door saleswomen.

"I'm Susan Van Dine, and this is my friend Catherine Synge," I explained. "You must be Ms. Fleck."

She was a tall, angular woman, in her fifties, with a haircut that looked like it had been done with a bowl and a dull pair of scissors. Her dress did not quite fit her. It hung on her like it was someone else's and she had just thrown it on when we rang the bell. She wore Birkenstock sandals with white athletic socks. The picture she made was not my idea of a personal secretary.

"Oh, of course," she said, stepping aside to let us by. "Please, come in."

While she closed the door, we stood quietly in the foyer. It was lined with paintings, landscapes mostly, probably British. There was a long Persian wool runner leading down the hall to two doors at the end.

"I was only expecting you, Susan," she said, emphasizing the "you." She looked a bit flushed, like someone who has discovered she has more dinner guests than dinner and is quietly calculating how to stretch it.

"Catherine's a historian," I explained. "I thought she could keep me on track so we don't waste any time."

Emily led us down the hall to one of the doors, which was slightly ajar. "If it goes well," she said, pushing it open, "you can come back."

The room we entered was very bright and overly warm, like they had the heat on already, even though it was only October. I didn't see anyone at first, because everything was very white and yellow and she blended right in. But on the white wicker chair near the front window with a big, cream-colored afghan thrown over her lap sat a very old woman, probably the oldest woman I'd ever seen. My own grandmother was only seventy-eight, and, like Tuttie, was still spry and lively. This woman was dozing in her chair, her skin as white as her hair, her hands folded loosely across her chest. She made a small snuffling noise as she slept. She did not hear us come in but woke only when Emily called her name.

"Elinor," she said softly, motioning us toward a big yellow couch next to Elinor's chair. "Miss Van Dine is here."

Elinor's eyes opened slowly, but she did not lift her head. She examined us from a forty-five degree tilt for several minutes, then, when she was thoroughly awake, adjusted herself in the chair.

"Which one is she?" Elinor asked at last.

"I'm Susan Van Dine," I said, standing up and extending a hand to her, "and this is a friend of mine, Catherine Synge."

She had an amazingly firm grip. I had expected a weak, dish towel sort of handshake, but she took my hand firmly and pulled it down with a strong tug.

Awake, she did not seem so fragile. She sat straight in the chair and tossed the afghan to one side.

"Bloody hot in here, Fleck," she said, taking Catherine and me by surprise by her tone and language. "My secretary," she said, turning to us with a conspiratorial whisper, "is terrified of my taking cold and dying of pneumonia. So it is always eighty or ninety degrees in here. It's like a bloody sauna."

Fleck had disappeared and come back with a tea tray. I glanced at my watch, concerned about the time.

"I've been anxious to meet you, Ms. Devere," I began, taking the teacup offered to me and passing it to Catherine. "Ms. Fleck has told you I'm doing some research on Lucy Weir."

"What?" she said, sipping at her tea. "Oh, yes, yes, of course she did." She sipped again noisily. She did not have the manners I associated with British aristocracy.

I pulled the scrapbook out of my knapsack. I had brought it along at Catherine's suggestion.

"We thought if you looked at some pictures we have," Catherine explained, "you'd remember some of the events they represent and tell us a bit about them."

Elinor frowned. "I don't need pictures to remind me," she scowled. "I have a perfect memory. I remember those days like they were yesterday. I can tell you every detail. You know, this is the same house I lived in then. Fleck wasn't with me then, she came just a bit before my Sarah died. This isn't the same furniture either, though some of it is. Sarah never liked yellow, but it cheers me up. Yellow is my favorite color, in fact. Then red. The bright colors. The fiery ones. I'm a fire sign, you see."

It was odd to hear a ninety-one-year-old talk about fire signs. Catherine and I both gently tried to interrupt her monologue about colors, but we could tell she was going to be hard to focus. Her memory may have been intact, but it wandered all over the room, bouncing off corners and turning into something entirely different. After fifteen minutes, though, she was lively and animated and Fleck let her go on for another fifteen. In fact, she kept extending the interview, till we had been there almost an hour and knew a lot of details but not much substance. We heard the story of meeting Sarah. We found out about her home in England, what Grove Street was like in 1920 when she first saw it, exactly what color Sarah's eyes were, and how long it took to cross the Atlantic in those days. "A jolly good time," she said.

When she began to look tired, I posed a final question. "Could you tell me how you found my shop? It seems so coincidental. Here I am, researching your old friend, and you wander into my store!"

Elinor clicked her tongue, suddenly more animated. "I would never just wander anywhere! I *knew* where we were going!"

Fleck, Catherine and I exchanged glances, and the two of them looked noticeably uncomfortable. "How?" I ventured.

Her voice lowered to a conspiratorial whisper. "It was rather like a dream," she said slowly. "I was sitting here and suddenly I saw myself entering your shop and buying that pin. Fleck thinks I've gone daft, but that's just how it happened. It was like someone or something compelled me to go there. This will sound odd, but I almost thought I heard Lucy's voice."

"I believe you," I said, and considering all that had happened to me, I *did* believe her.

Elinor liked us that first day. I could tell. In fact, she called after us, "Come back soon!" as Fleck escorted us back out to the foyer.

"She's a strange one," Fleck said simply, "hard to pin down. It's her age. She didn't used to ramble so. Or have these revelations she says she has."

We left, a little confused and dazed by an hour of loosely connected memories. Catherine felt challenged; I was just tired.

"We didn't find out a thing that we need, really," I sighed.

"It's like that," Catherine smiled. "It's hard work sometimes."

"I wonder if it's worth it," I said, thinking I might have more luck just rummaging through Lucy's box.

"Oh, it's always worth it. Think of it, even if she is a little crazy—she knew Lucy Weir," Catherine said, kissing me on the cheek before we went off in opposite directions. "It's worth it. You'll see."

♦

We went back to visit Elinor the following Sunday, and, knowing what she was like, had planned our method of attack more carefully. She was seated in the same room, the same chair, with the same afghan over her, as if she'd been waiting there all week for our return. In fact, she said, "Well, it's about time," as we came in and sat across from her.

Catherine pulled out the scrapbook and flipped to a photo of Harriet and Lucy in their apartment. "You remember Harriet Timberlake, of course," Catherine said.

"Of course I do!" But her tone was coldly, rather than warmly, reminiscent.

"She was an actress," I inserted. "Do you remember much about her acting career?"

"Hrmph," Elinor said, burrowing her chin into the afghan. "An actress, indeed!"

Catherine and I exchanged a quick and puzzled look. We had never expected discord in The Gang. From the photos of warm, smiling faces, we had assumed a camaraderie, a pocket of lesbian friends who traveled together, supported each others' work. Hadn't Sarah mischievously autographed her book "For my partners in crime"? Where was the chill in Elinor's voice coming from?

"She *was* an actress?" I asked cautiously. "We have evidence of that. She played in regional theaters, possibly a few movies. Is that correct?"

"Oh, of course, if you call that acting," Elinor frowned, taking the teacup Fleck offered her. "Lucy was always after her to pursue the legitimate theater, to act Shakespeare and the classics. But Harriet went for light, romantic drivel. Drawing room comedies. Movies that were made in a few weeks, the kind that only played a day in each theater. Plays that were so badly written they offended the intellect. She never made any money at it. Or what she made she quickly spent on clothes for all the parties she went to. She was a bit wild, never really grew up."

Elinor started losing the grip of her teacup; she was falling asleep even as she spoke to us. I asked another question to try to wake her up and prolong the session.

"But they were happy together, weren't they?"

"Oh," she said, pulling the afghan closer around her, "at first I suppose. By the time I met them, though, they'd settled into their roles. Harriet always running about, Lucy writing and teaching, making money. Lucy was always working. Those photos, they're mostly of places we went to, following Harriet's so-called career. Lucy was worried, you see, and started following Harriet to her various performances. It consumed so much of her time, working and following Harriet, that it took her away from other things. Like the women's club she had been a member of, Heterodoxy. Though perhaps that wasn't such a loss, ultimately. Sarah remained active in it for years, till around 1927, I believe, when the atmosphere became more conservative in the club. Helen Hull—you must have heard her name? the novelist?—and Sarah had a dreadful experience at a meeting in which another member had the cheek to define the 'perfect feminist' as a wife and mother! When they took objection and no one would back them up, they began to be disillusioned with the group. Things narrowed so, the group changed, and Sarah found other things to do."

"And the performances you spoke of?" I asked, to get back to Lucy and Harriet. "Did you go along? Is that what all the group photos in Lucy's album were about?"

"Oh yes, Sarah and I went along with Lucy quite a bit, went to see the most dreadful plays you can imagine. If they could be called plays. Sarah and I went to good theater in

New York, and to the Provincetown Players, which was very au courant. Saw a lot of O'Neill's early plays. And the four of us saw *The Captive* with Helen Mencken in 1926. You know what that was, don't you?"

I didn't, but Catherine of course did, and explained that it was a Broadway play with lesbian content that was closed by the police for its supposed immorality. The star, Helen Mencken, who later married Humphrey Bogart, went to jail temporarily, and the play created a furor that led to the passing of the padlock law, which prohibited the portrayal of homosexuals on the New York stage until 1967.

"We were there on opening night," Elinor elaborated, and though it was off the subject, it was fascinating nonetheless. "Most of the audience was young women like us, in pairs or groups. We never had such an opportunity before to see a play that spoke directly to us, to be in such a group of women. It was one of the most moving experiences of that decade for me, perhaps of my life."

"I can't help but notice," I said cautiously, well aware that I should not antagonize my interviewee, "that you're a bit disdainful of Harriet."

Catherine poked me with her index finger. I pulled away and continued looking straight at Elinor.

"She was never my favorite person," Elinor said, coughing into the afghan. "If it hadn't been for Lucy, we would never have been friends with her at all, Sarah and I. But Sarah loved Lucy so, they were both writers and politically aware, and I was immensely fond of her also. She was such a *good* person, a caring person. Helped Sarah and me patch things up more than once, I'd say. She was fair and even-tempered. Her one blind spot was Harriet, and I must admit I never understood it. Oh, Harriet was pretty enough, and when she wanted to be, she could be charming. But she was such a flirtatious, frivolous thing. Why, she even tried flirting with my Sarah. She didn't know how to be friendly, really. If she liked you, then she'd flirt." She coughed again, and I thought she was finished, but she went on with a raspy voice. "I can't say I was torn up when she died."

"But Lucy was, I assume?" I asked, startled by her bluntness.

"Yes, she went practically dotty," Elinor continued, pushing her teacup toward Fleck for a refill. The tea was lukewarm now, and she drank her second cup in one long swallow. "Ah!" she sighed. "Good tea."

"I've heard she went away for a while," I pursued, trying to keep her on track. She was fading again, and I still had questions.

"Hmm? Yes, yes, for a while, I can't remember exactly. Maybe for a month," she said, but her eyelids looked heavy. Elinor had grown sad-looking and was now resting her chin on her chest. Soon after, she dozed off, and Fleck escorted us out.

♦

After we left Elinor's, Catherine and I briefly considered spending the evening with each other. We walked to the subway together, where Catherine would go in one direction and I in another. We stood at the token booth, stalling for time, looking for our tokens in our pockets, thinking of bits of news we hadn't told each other, waiting for one or the other to make the first move. But neither could or would. We passed through the turnstile finally and waved reluctantly goodbye.

That night in bed, I read some of Harriet's letters to Lucy. One was written from Provincetown and was full of praise for a fellow actress, Amelia Wingate. Harriet, I gathered, was touring for several weeks with a regional theater group. The play, she herself acknowledged, was dreadful, but the acting company was marvelous.

I don't know when I fell asleep or how the lights got turned off. I didn't want to explore the possibilities at the time. But I woke to a sudden pressure on the mattress of someone sitting down carefully on the edge, trying not to disturb me. I nearly jumped off the bed with fright.

"It is only I," someone said, precisely and correctly, and I recognized the level clarity of Lucy's voice. "You're hearing things about Harriet, from someone who didn't particularly care for her. Elinor is a fine person, but she could never see Harriet's good points."

"But," I began, and my voice failed me. It was like a dream I often had, in which I faced some danger and tried to speak but couldn't. Before I could find my voice, the mattress had straightened out again and I knew I was alone in the bed.

But Lucy, I wanted to say, were you happy? I decided there was no way to really know, unless I looked for the answers in the box.

◆ 20 ◆

August, 1930

We met in an unusual way.

I received a letter from my sister Edith in Glens Falls, asking me to join her and her husband at the races in Saratoga one weekend. I was not much for horse racing, it held no particular interest for me, so I wrote back and declined but said I would be pleased to visit her in Glens Falls sometime in the fall. She wrote again, most insistent, saying that she had arranged a very important meeting for me there and would I kindly not embarrass her by not showing up. So I took the train to Saratoga on Friday morning. It was August, several weeks before my classes at Barnard resumed. I was at that time finishing the novel that would become *Central Park*, my first, a horrid little thing about a male professor and his love affair with a female student. It was my first and only stab at writing about such things. I did indeed need a break from it, and it was hard not to obey my older sister.

I took a room at the Saratoga House, which was my favorite at that time, being cozier and less expensive than the Grand Union or the United States. Also, it was run by a Jewish family, and was the only hotel in town not displaying the offensive "No Jews or Dogs Admitted" sign. Once I did stay at the Grand Union and was quite disappointed. It was certainly grand on the outside, with its impressive veranda running an entire city block. But the inside was dingy, low-ceilinged and filled with worn-out Victorian furniture. I ate in the famous dining room, bigger than anything I'd ever seen, only to find my table wobbly and the linen soiled. For this they charged as much as forty dollars a day for a room!

So I preferred the Saratoga House, which was smaller and better kept. It was also filled with old furniture, which at least did not tip over. I had taken before, and got again, the corner room on the third floor, which was a little larger than the others and had a nice view up Broadway.

I arranged to meet my sister for dinner. Her husband Matthew was coming down the next day from Glens Falls, and she did not like to dine alone. I talked her into dinner at my hotel, though she would have much preferred one of the others. I believe they were staying at the United States. Edith was quite pretentious. She was from a small town, married to a small-town businessman, but she wanted to rub elbows with the elite of New York.

"What is the purpose of staying in Saratoga," she said, "if we can't be seen in the best places?"

Of course, I had the feeling I knew what the "important meeting" was that she had arranged. She was very vague about it at dinner, saying only that it would change my life and might even rescue me from New York. I reminded her that I liked New York and had been very lucky to acquire a position at Barnard at my age. I was at that time just twenty-seven years old and had spent most of my life in small towns like Glens Falls, where I grew up, and Saratoga, where I had gone to college and then taught. I had been in New York for two years and for the first time felt unrestrained and unfettered by small-town conventions. Nothing was going to take me away.

Especially not what Edith had in mind. My suspicions were confirmed the next morning as we were enjoying breakfast at the track. There was no racing that early, but we had a wonderful view from the clubhouse of the horses' morning trot. We were joined by Matthew and his business associate, Richard Pleasant. He was exactly that.

I was polite as usual. I was, after all, not angry at Mr. Pleasant, who smiled at me harmlessly and unknowingly across the scrambled eggs. It was actually rather brave of him to meet his business partner's old maid sister-in-law. I wonder that the pressure didn't make him bolt. I think I would have, in his shoes. But he was charmingly calm and talkative right through the final cup of coffee. My sister smiled effusively, and she was the one I could have throttled.

I had not come right out and told her my feelings on the subject of men, but I think she could have guessed. I had had, by that time, a number of close friendships with women, including Mary Strickland, my teacher and mentor at Skidmore. We had lived together for several years. I would have, in fact, still been in Saratoga if she had not taken up with an older woman—her teacher and mentor, who came back to retire in Saratoga after many years of teaching at Smith. It was partially a broken heart that took me to New York.

Edith, though, in her self-imposed blindness, insisted that I was just a career woman who had not met the right man. She had, over the years, tried to find him for me. It was clear after this latest episode that I was going to have to set her straight. It was unfair to me and to all the Mr. Pleasants who had had to endure brief, gratingly polite meals with me.

In the middle of the day, I told Edith the heat was affecting me and that I had to go lie down. She seemed to believe that, as did Mr. Pleasant, who had heard as much about women's propensity to fainting as I had. Mr. Pleasant offered to escort me back to the hotel, and it must have seemed extraordinarily brazen to refuse, when I think about it now. Women just did not go about unescorted in those days, as they do now, especially not in a slightly seedy gambling town like Saratoga.

Back in town, there was a lot of excitement on Broadway just down the street from my hotel. One block was cordoned off to traffic. An enormous crowd of people had gathered in front of the Broadway Theater. At first I thought it must be for the latest matinee, but as I got closer, it was a most interesting sight. On the sidewalk in front of the theater were two moving picture cameras, and a crew of red-faced men controlling the crowds with megaphones. A man holding a ragged manuscript was talking closely to a man aiming one of the cameras, waving the script at him in an animated way, shouting "No! No! No!" above the hum of the crowd. As I wedged my way through to the front, I caught sight of the actor, a dashing dark-haired idol I was sure I had seen on film before. Next to him, fanning herself and calling for a touchup to her makeup, was Harriet.

There was nothing very special about her looks. She was undeniably pretty, in the way of most actresses of the day, coquettish and slightly pouty. Her mannerisms were that of a spoiled child. When she brushed wisps of her sandy-colored hair from her face or adjusted the sash of her dress, it was with a dramatic, affected air.

But there was a second after her makeup was freshened when she peered into the crowd, assessing what people thought of her. In her eyes was written a question, that of her own worth. I caught those eyes with mine and smiled broadly. Later she said that I winked, but I can't imagine that I did. Whatever I did, she smiled back, the question removed. Standing there in her virginal white dress, her hair falling carelessly over her shoulders, she looked almost shy. She waited patiently for the scene to be filmed. She did it beautifully, a model of dramatic poise and ability.

I remained standing there, after the crowd had cleared. I walked up to her bravely as the crew began to pack up the equipment.

"Is this your first photoplay?" I asked politely. She smiled, casting down her eyes, then half looking up at me again.

"How could you tell?" she blushed.

"You seemed uncertain at first," I said. "But then you performed beautifully."

"Thank you," she said, simply.

"I'm Lucy Weir," I said, "and I'd be pleased to have you join me for dinner tonight. If you tell me your hotel and room, I'll ring you up."

"Oh," she said, looking suddenly embarrassed. "Well, I, you see, don't have a hotel. I mean, I live in town. With my family. Well, you see, it's a local photoplay, I got the part when I starred in a pageant earlier this month."

I realized then she was no more than twenty.

"Then perhaps you'll meet me at the Saratoga House anyway," I insisted, charmed at her discomfort. "For dinner at six o'clock."

She nodded, raising those clear eyes to meet mine squarely. "Of course," she said. "That would be lovely."

"I'll see you then, Miss —?" I said, realizing I had awkwardly not asked her name.

"Timberlake," she smiled. "Harriet Timberlake."

♦

It was quite a risk I had taken, and as I dressed to go down to dinner, I could not imagine why I had done so. I could lose my position at Barnard. But there was something in her eyes, I told myself, something that spoke to a feeling we could not ignore.

As I straightened my skirt and buttoned my jacket in front of the mirror in my room, something else was troubling me. I caught my own eyes in the mirror. At the corners, when I talked or smiled, were the beginnings of crow's feet. I had four grey hairs mixed in with the auburn. My waist had thickened to twenty-eight inches in the last year. My suit, though it fit well, was a dull, dowdy beige.

"You're an old maid," I said to my reflection, thinking of the sprightly Harriet, in her girlish dress, probably not too long out of high school. At the last minute, I added a dot of rouge to my cheeks and stuck a posey in my lapel.

The funny thing was, Harriet had had the same anxiety, only in reverse. It was apparent the moment I saw her at dinner. In fact, I hardly recognized her. She wore a somber, dark blue serge suit even though it was August. Her long, wavy hair was tucked up neatly under her straw skimmer, and she was battling with a few stray wisps before she saw me. She was fidgeting with her gloves also, pulling them up and smoothing the fingers as if they were too small or she had borrowed them from someone else. Except for her face, she looked as old as I.

But of course, I thought, she dressed for a meeting with a maiden teacher.

We were oddly formal with each other during dinner. I ordered the roast beef, and Harriet the baked chicken. She hardly touched her food. I, as always, ate heartily, and commented on her lack of appetite.

"I want to be in photoplays," she explained, "and the camera adds such weight to you, you wouldn't believe. I looked like a fat woman in my screen test!"

It was one of the longest things she said at dinner. Mostly, I asked her questions and she answered them briefly, often with her eyes cast down. When I talked about myself, she looked up and smiled charmingly. It was a bit like dining with one of my students.

At the end, over coffee and a raspberry ice she let melt in the dish, she offered me her first question of the evening.

"How long will you be staying?"

Since I had assumed I was boring her, her interest was touching.

"I leave tomorrow morning," I answered. "The races don't appeal to me, and I have classes to prepare for."

"Oh, I see," she said, drawing a calling card from her pocketbook, an address book, and an elegant fountain pen. "May I write to you? Would you give me your address?" She held out the book and pen for me to write it down.

"That would be fine," I said, surprised by her interest. "I mean, I would like that." When I finished, she handed me one of her cards to keep. I had to resist the urge to run my finger over the embossed gold of "Miss Harriet Timberlake."

"This is a lovely pen," I said instead, rubbing my hand over it. "It has a nice feel to it."

"My father brought it back from Italy," she said, closing her pocketbook. "I hardly use it. Perhaps you'd like to keep it?"

I was startled and handed it ungraciously across the table. "I couldn't," I said. "It was a gift, and, I'm sure, an expensive one."

I knew it was a mistake by the way she cast her eyes down and plopped the pen carelessly into her bag. She sighed instead of speaking.

Then in such an intimate tone I surprised both of us, I half whispered, "Write me something beautiful with it." She looked up, her head tilted rakishly to one side, and smiled seductively.

"I will," she said, with a soft blush rising in her cheeks.

Later, alone in my room, I did what I had resisted earlier. I sat on the edge of the bed with her calling card in my left hand, my right index finger feeling the silky bumps of her name. I am embarrassed to admit that I took off my suit and shirtwaist and stood again in front of the mirror in my petticoat and chemise. I let my hair down over my shoulders and brushed it till it shone. I let one strap of my chemise fall over my shoulder and stared in wonder at the creamy smoothness of my own skin.

Harriet Timberlake wanted me, I could tell. Maybe she was too young to know what that meant, but it seemed unlikely. And I was suddenly no longer Miss Weir, the spinster schoolteacher. I was Lucy, and I was desired.

◆ 21 ◆

August, 1930

I remember receiving that first letter from her. I knew, instinctively it seems, that it had been written with the Italian fountain pen. When I saw the return address, my heart began to race, my palms to perspire. "Miss Harriet Timberlake, Union Avenue, Saratoga Springs." I left it sitting on the dressing table for hours, unopened. I wanted to prolong the moment of first seeing it, first touching it, first lifting it to my face and smelling the unmistakable scent of Harriet. Roses, it smelled magnificently of roses. Fresh cut, June roses.

I opened it finally, after hurriedly preparing for my next day's classes (and distractedly—did I teach them anything that day, those bright, eager faces? Or did they stare out at me from their desks, puzzled by our sudden leap from Milton to the Romantics?). In bed, I lay the letter shamelessly on the pillow beside me. I read it through five times quickly before I let the words register. "My dear Miss Weir," I read, not "Miss Weir" or "Dear Miss Weir," but *her* dear Miss Weir.

How did she know that I, too, felt the bond between us instantly? How did she know that I could not describe or explain it either, that if I had let myself, I also might have thought we had both led past lives? But not I, rational, somber Lucy Weir! I could not indulge myself in those popular beliefs and practices—past lives, seances, Ouija boards—but oh, oh how the temptation to find the answer was there! Were we man and woman in another time? Husband and wife? Star-crossed lovers? Lifelong companions? Old maids together?

"May I hope to be your friend?" she asked.

My dear, oh my dear, you may hope to be much more!

♦

I responded immediately, writing that I would like nothing better than to meet her again when she visited New York. It was forever till I heard from her again. This was, of course, 1917 and wartime, and the mails traveled much less quickly than they do now. When I think about it, it seems such a long time ago, such an ancient time. There were so few automobiles in the city then, so many more horses. I took a horse-drawn streetcar to visit Harriet. Eighty-fifth Street, where we later moved, was still somewhat of a frontier, and Barnard was seemingly in another country. In those days, I lived in one room in a building on West 101st Street, what was called a bed/sitting room. I shared a hall bath with three other unmarried women. I could have invited Harriet to my room, as she was a woman and it would never have been seen as out of the ordinary, but it did not seem the proper place. I had nowhere to make coffee or tea, and the atmosphere was not conducive to entertaining guests. So, like a gentleman caller, I arranged to meet her for lunch at her aunt's house in Gramercy Park.

We were shy with each other. Harriet barely spoke at first and hesitated to look directly at me, though several times I caught her eye. I was introduced to her mother and her aunt, who both looked me over curiously as if they could not discern why a woman of my age was pursuing a friendship with a girl of Harriet's years. I wanted them to believe I had taken a teacher's interest in her, that I might, given my familiarity with Shakespeare and the classics, influence her toward a career on the legitimate stage and away from the moving pictures. In fact, the talk at lunch was much in that direction. Mrs. McClelland, Harriet's aunt, had briefly been on the stage herself, at the turn of the century, but had abandoned it when she met her husband. She, too, had studied with Theodora Winkler, with whom Harriet would now take lessons.

The plan, as she revealed it, was that Harriet would live with the McClellands and study every day with Madame Winkler and twice a week with an elocution instructor, who would soften the rough edges of her accent.

I couldn't help wondering, as I watched her daintily nibbling at her chicken with as little appetite as the last time we'd met, what Harriet wanted. Was she excited by the prospect of living in New York and taking acting lessons? Or did she have reservations? When we were finally alone in the parlor having coffee, I asked her. Her answer came out in a rush of emotion and with several tears.

"It all seems so silly," she said. "I want to be an actress, and a good one, but to study every day? I just want to *act.*"

I found myself patting her arm, then her hand, and she lay her hand gently over mine. It became unbearably warm in the room and I flushed and lowered my face to hide my embarrassment. She stood and placed an arm around my shoulders, as if to comfort *me*, when she was the one who needed comfort. It was a moment that touched me deeply.

"I'm so glad to have you here," she said softly, as if I were her oldest and dearest friend in all the world, when, in fact, we barely knew each other. "I will be so happy to be in the same city with you!"

We talked then, long and fully, about ourselves, our dreams and aspirations. She was, I knew, like me, a woman meant to have a full life, her own life, a woman who would never tie herself to a man. It was late when her mother came in to interrupt us; the afternoon light was fading. We parted, but with plans to meet the next day for a walk.

It was, as I recall and as I have carried it with me these many years, one of the most purely happy afternoons of my life.

♦

During the next month, we saw each other as often as we could, though never enough. Because I was a sort of mentor, a respected college instructor, I was invited to Gramercy Park for dinner on several occasions, but always as the dinner companion for an eligible bachelor or widower who was a friend of the family. I am certain that Mrs. McClelland wondered about my unmarried status. I was not considered a bad-looking woman. Though unmarried school teachers have never been an unusual breed, a woman without a man was still subject to question. Was I a suffragette, Harriet's uncle wanted to know? Written beneath the question was another: Was I going to influence his niece in that direction?

I was not a vociferous proponent of votes for women, though I, of course, did support the cause, and it was the principal reason I had been drawn to become a member of Heterodoxy, a women's club that met in Greenwich Village. The McClellands, however, did not understand the nature of that group, and I was purposefully vague about its meetings, labeling it a "social group," though we were all at that time self-described feminists. Many of us had socialist leanings. I didn't mention the names of the famous and politically vocal members whom Mr. McClelland would surely have recognized— Crystal Eastman, Katharine Anthony, Inez Haynes Irwin—or the many others I had met or who had spoken at our meetings, like Rose Schneiderman, who would not have won the approval of Mr. McClelland, a banker with Morgan Guaranty. The less he knew, I thought, the better, though when he asked direct questions, I responded just as directly.

Which became my undoing. One evening at dinner, in front of Mrs. McClelland, Mr. Carmody, a young and unmarried banker, and Harriet and her cousin Priscilla, who was Harriet's age, Mr. McClelland, in a confrontational mood, told the story of a secretary in his office who made an error typing some figures and caused the bank considerable embarrassment vis-à-vis an important client. "So," ended Mr. McClelland, "it is clear why women do not deserve the same treatment as men. They simply do not have the heads for grave matters such as finances or politics."

I would have smiled wanly, to keep the peace, and hoped the topic shifted quickly, had he not attempted to engage me in the discussion.

"Given this example, don't you agree, Miss Weir?"

I swallowed noisily and glanced for help toward Harriet, who was well aware of my political leanings. I had described to her in depth my first political rally, a mass meeting three years before at Cooper Union on the subject, "What Is Feminism," where I had met Marie Howe, the founder of Heterodoxy. How I had thrilled to hear such wonderful speakers as Crystal Eastman and Floyd Dell divulge their thoughts on the meaning of feminism! Marie Howe's words had echoed with me for days: "We intend to be our whole, big, human selves." What was I to say to Mr. McClelland, given how I felt?

I replied honestly that I did not agree, could not, that I failed to understand how he could make a generalization about women from one incident. I went on to discuss women's numerous competencies, as proven in the war effort. Where, I questioned, would the country be without the women ambulance drivers, the female munitions workers? What would come from women's war work, I hoped, was the recognition that they did indeed deserve every political and economic right and privilege afforded to men.

Mr. McClelland grew red in the face, his wife rang the bell for the maid to clear, even though Mr. Carmody was still eating. Harriet smiled at me sheepishly. She knew all too well what would follow. I was not to be invited back. Harriet was restricted from seeing me, on the basis of my "radical and inflammatory" ideas. My calls to her went unanswered. I wrote her letters that were returned unopened, though, I knew, Harriet had never seen them. For several weeks, we both endured this torment.

It was in sheer desperation one evening that Harriet arrived at my room, carrying her leather suitcase, the one her parents had given her when she left Saratoga. Her eyes were red and blotchy and she kept pulling a handkerchief out of her sleeve to blow her nose.

"My parents want me back in Saratoga," she whimpered. "They say New York is bad for me, that it makes me despondent. But I am only so because I can't see you!"

I found strength for both of us. I held her tenderly in my

arms and calmed her as best I could. When she stopped crying, we sat quietly on the bed, her hand in mine so small and cold, and we discussed the only possible solution. That is how Harriet left home, and how we came to live together, first in Greenwich Village, and later on Eighty-fifth Street.

♦ 22 ♦

The sun was just coming up as I finished reading. I had read and reread the August 1930 installments hungrily and happily, content in and thrilled by the knowledge that Lucy and Harriet had been totally in love at the beginning. Her words brought the two of them off the page to me in the same way the photographs had. I was suddenly there with them in Saratoga, at the next table, watching the two shy women fall in love over chicken and roast beef. I had chosen the chicken also and was eating it in tiny, quiet bites, so conscious that the sound of my own chewing could drown out their hushed voices. At the moment Lucy whispered, "Write me something beautiful with it," I swallowed so loudly I was sure they would turn to stare at me. But they were so absorbed with each other they never heard me, never saw me, in fact I think I must have only dreamt that I was there. Yet in the light of the new day, I had a curious taste in my mouth, like baked chicken.

I had not been up and around so early in a long time, yet I couldn't fall back asleep. After the second installment in the journal, there was tucked a thin, yellowed envelope, containing half a dozen photographs. They were not of the Eighty-fifth Street apartment, which I had seen in the scrapbook, but of Harriet and Lucy in a much smaller place, which was labeled on the back of the photos as "Bank Street." Probably, I reasoned, their first apartment together. The pictures showed them in a crowded parlor, with books lining the walls and floors and several overstuffed chairs circling a small tea table.

The wallpaper was an old-fashioned and gaudy Edwardian print that clashed with the upholstery of the chairs. A heavy curtain hung on one wall, probably separating the parlor from the bedroom. But both of them looked out at me happily from the pictures, cramped but obviously in love.

Also in the envelope were several receipts from the early 1920s, showing income Lucy received from selling stories to magazines—not famous ones, but obscure names like *The Listener* and *The Ladies' Library*. She was prolific, and the checks amounted to several thousand dollars. I wondered if they had been their ticket to a larger apartment.

I read on in the journal, but the story of Harriet and Lucy was abruptly broken off. What followed were heavily edited essays about the craft of writing. The journal seemed to be a catchall, not just for reminiscences, but for all sorts of ruminations. Needless to say, I found them less interesting than the breathtaking writing about Harriet.

So after a while, I called Catherine. She was still sound asleep, and she was too groggy to recognize my familiar "Hi." I had to add quickly, "It's Susan."

"Hi, Susan," she repeated, still asleep, though within seconds I could tell she had woken up and realized she had the receiver in her hand. "Oh, Susan," she yawned in recognition. "What time is it?"

"Six twenty-nine," I said, wondering what I was going to say next.

"Six twenty-nine," she said after me. "Is something the matter?"

Something *was* the matter, wasn't it? Why wasn't she sleeping next to me? Why wasn't her soft hair fanned out over the pillow, and where were her endearing sleep noises? What had happened to us? And most importantly, was there any way to stop it from continuing? Could we be equal partners and accept each other's take on life without losing ourselves?

"I just read two parts of Lucy's journal," I said, in a burst of emotion. "She wrote them in 1930, maybe as a sort of autobiography, about how she and Harriet met and fell in love and began living together. There are pictures of them in their first apartment together. It all made me think of you, and I wanted to tell you."

"Oh, Susan," she said, and I could tell she was sincerely touched. "That's very nice."

"Do you remember when we met?" I asked. "How I fumbled around after a meeting, asking you out, and you said no?"

"But I apologized and said yes later," Catherine elaborated. "I was a little intimidated by you. All those degrees. Obviously a different class of girl. And I was ashamed of liking someone in business school. Like it was morally wrong or something. But secretly, I thought it was great to be so at ease with numbers, when I never was. I was terrified of money."

That was the first time Catherine had ever let on that I had impressed her as much as she had me. I suddenly felt flushed.

I couldn't help myself; I had to go on now that we'd started. "I'm not sure what went wrong with us, but I'm willing to try to figure it out," I blurted out. "I'd... do you think... do you want to have a date this week? A real date? Maybe Wednesday?"

I could see her smile through the telephone wire. I could see her twisting her hair in thought, now totally awake, trying to decide what she should do with this crazy lover who talked to dead women and had become, in a few short months, a pathological liar. I could see her tottering on the brink of indecision, tempted yet knowing better. Finally, she crashed over the edge and landed, feet first, as always.

"Friday would be better for me," she said simply.

"Then Friday it is," I said, and we hung up soon after. It was the beginning of one of the more hopeful days I'd had recently.

♦

When the mail came that day at the shop, there was a letter from Mrs. Roger Timberlake. It was on heavy, light blue vellum paper with her name embossed in coordinating dark blue ink. She wrote in a small, precise hand:

Dear Miss Van Dine,

Your visit stirred many memories for me of my late husband. After you left, I went back through boxes I hadn't touched since he passed away. I found in our attic the scrapbook I told you about, the one he kept with clippings of his Aunt Harriet. I have looked through it carefully, and I suspect it would be of great interest to you. I have a sincere distrust of the mail and am hesitant to let the book out of my sight. As you can guess, because my husband kept it as a boy, it has great sentimental value. If you would like to see it, please call me and perhaps we can arrange a time to meet on one of your next trips to Saratoga.

Sincerely yours,

Evelyn Timberlake (Mrs. Roger)

I was tempted to jump in the station wagon that day, but it was Tuttie's day off and I was clearly supposed to make an appointment with Mrs. Timberlake in advance. The trip would have to wait, maybe as much as a week. But the existence of Roger Timberlake's boyhood scrapbook buoyed me: the pieces were going to slip into place, and it remained to be seen what picture the finished puzzle would make.

♦

"Tuttie," I said on Friday afternoon, "I'm nervous as a kid before her first date."

"Getting back together is hard, sweetie," she said. "I did it once, with Leonard Rosenthal. We went together for a year or two, and I broke if off because I thought he was getting too serious, you know, like he was gonna propose. But I missed him a lot, so after a couple of months, we hitched up again." Her voice trailed off, even though it seemed like there was more to tell.

"What happened?" I prompted.

"Oh, babycakes, you don't want to know that," she said, flushing a little, I thought. She was probably thinking her story wasn't such a good idea after all.

"Sure I do," I persisted.

"Well," and she cleared her throat, "it only lasted a week. Maybe two, tops. But it was a swell time," she added hastily. "Non-stop whoopie—if you know what I mean." She winked conspiratorially, and I smiled in spite of the message of her story. "Not that it won't last for you and that little dumpling of yours. You got something much more than me and old Lennie had."

"Yeah?" I said, brightening. "What?"

"Chemistry," she said. "Just the right kind. H_2O. CO_2. You know, cupcake, the stuff that makes the world go 'round."

I was beaming, but more from my affection for Tuttie than from her words of encouragement. At that moment in time I considered myself truly lucky. I had known Margielove. I had been lovers with Catherine Synge. And I counted among my best friends Tuttie Posner.

Catherine insisted that I pick the spot, and I chose the White Horse Tavern in the Village, because it was the first place I thought of when I thought of romance. Not because of its decor or menu, because it really was just an old tavern with ponderous wooden tables and frosty mugs of beer. But I associated it with great literary figures, the giants of literature who had drunk themselves into a stupor there, like Dylan Thomas, whose favorite table is commemorated with a plaque. Catherine was amused at my choice and said she was hungry for a hamburger, so it was a good choice. She thought it appropriate that I'd selected a place haunted by literary ghosts.

We didn't get Dylan Thomas' table, but we had a nice table in the corner just the same. We ordered burgers and mugs of Bass Ale and sat nervously playing with the condiments on the table, both afraid of why we'd come together like this.

"Cath—"

"Sus—"

They came out at the same time, and we both laughed and tried again. Since the evening was my idea, Catherine deferred to me.

"This is hard," I smiled, not sure if I meant the moment or the whole evening. The waitress plunked our beers down, and we had something else to distract us from talking. I took a long drink of beer and started again.

"I don't know why this is so hard," I said, weakly, and Catherine broke in to save me from my own ineptitude.

"I've missed you, Susan," she said sadly. "And every day I ask myself why I miss you. You're so weird and fucked up. You talk to dead women, and you're convinced they talk to you. You've lied to me more than anyone ever has. You're not especially political, and you're privileged and over-educated. It's not just sex either. I know it's not just sex, because I've had great sex with other people. I just don't know why, but I have this overwhelming desire to be with you. It's like I'm compelled to, or something."

Did she really say all that, or have I dreamt it? Did my greatest fantasy really come spilling out of her like that? Or was I the one who did the gushing? It hardly matters now, though I like this way of remembering it. The reason it doesn't matter is that we ate and drank slowly, like people with all the time in the world. We talked about many things, especially how people in relationships become consumed with each other and how we needed to try to prevent that. How we had to find some way to accept each other's world view. How I had to assert my own thoughts and feelings more. Like people who know each other very well, we let the pauses come naturally and we didn't panic and rush to fill them in. Later, I went home with her. And later still, in the weeks that followed, we began our search for an apartment we could share.

◆

"She was unfaithful, of course!" Elinor blurted out on Sunday to my direct question about why Lucy had been worried enough to trail Harriet upstate and across New England. It was what I had always known, from the time in Saratoga, when Harriet took me into her confidence. "But she's faithful to me," Harriet had said with a smirk of pride that made me both hate and adore her. Still, I was stunned to hear it from someone else, someone living, someone who couldn't be brushed aside as the figment of an overactive imagination.

The truth is, I had painted an idealistic picture of Lucy and Harriet's relationship from the first day I'd seen the scrapbook. It had seemed the height of romance, these lesbians with arms entwined in resort towns, on sand dunes, in the quiet of their parlor. With their two best friends, their gang, they made a quartet I'd envied. I wanted such a group. What did it all mean if The Gang was only together to please Lucy, if Harriet and Lucy were not the Alice B. Toklas and Gertrude Stein of the Upper West Side, if one of their closest friends disliked one and felt sorry for the other? I remembered what Lucy had told me the other night, and I approached the topic now, looking for some last way to salvage the beautiful picture I'd had, which was yellowing and curling at the corners. Elinor was rambling on, rattling off the names of Harriet's many indiscretions.

"And Lucy," she finished, "was too lovestruck to care."

"And if she didn't," I asked, as politely as I could, "why did you?"

I didn't mean it to sound so confrontational, but it did, even in my ears. I knew as soon as I said it that I'd gone too far. Catherine tried to mend the break.

"What Susan means is. . ." she started, but Elinor raised up on her high horse.

"Don't you care when your friends are taken advantage of?" she said forcefully. "Don't you ever feel protective of someone you care for? I'm telling you, Harriet was practically without ethics. She would have had my Sarah, if Sarah hadn't had such a strong moral code!"

I touched something tender, I knew, a spot still raw sixty years later. And, though I wondered if she had ever tried to like Harriet, I sympathized with Elinor. I wouldn't like it much if a friend of mine hit on Catherine.

Fleck cleared her throat loudly, and it seemed to be time to leave. It was apparent from the set of Elinor's jaw that I'd angered her by questioning her loyalty and ethical code. And

I had to admit to myself, I'd overstepped the bounds of good interviewing techniques.

"I guess," Catherine said, as Fleck stood to show us out, "we'll see you next week." But even Catherine, the hopeful and tactful facilitator, couldn't patch it up.

"I'm finished talking about Harriet Timberlake," Elinor growled. "You needn't come back."

"But we still need to know. . ." I began, but she cut me off.

"You want something I can't give you," Elinor said. "I suggest you look for it elsewhere."

About Lucy, I wanted to finish. What happened to Lucy?

◆ 23 ◆

The leaves had almost finished falling the day I drove to Saratoga to visit Evelyn Timberlake. I went in mid-week, early in the morning, with plans to return that evening. Tuttie was ill with a head cold, so I had had to close the shop for the day.

Mrs. Timberlake was ready for me. She had laid out a tempting breakfast of coffee and danish pastries, and the scrapbook she had promised me rested invitingly next to me on the sofa. We ate first, as she described her search for the scrapbook. Since he had lived in this house all of his life, her husband Roger had never had occasion to prune his possessions, as other people do when they move from home to home. She had come across booties he had worn at one, hair he had had trimmed at four, teeth he had lost at six, valentines he had received at eight, exams he had taken at twelve. She had had to wade through his entire childhood to find the treasure I wanted to see.

"But it made me feel closer to him," she smiled at me. "Like time really is a continuum, is fluid somehow—that people die, but are still there in memory, or in the things they owned or made. I actually held my husband's baby teeth in my hand!" she said, stretching out her right hand to me then curling back the fingers slowly. "I can't tell you how that made me feel."

"I know what you mean," I nodded. "I feel that way every time I hold an antique. Though your feeling, of course," I added quickly, "is more personal."

"Um, yes," she agreed, drawing back her hand and tucking it beside her on the chair. "Well, shall we have a look-see?"

The talk of time and history made me slightly forgetful. For a second, I thought she wanted me to look at her husband's baby teeth with her. Then I remembered the scrapbook.

It was larger than the photo scrapbook I had of Lucy's, and it was from a slightly different time. Roger had apparently kept the clippings loose at first, perhaps in a box, then pasted them into the scrapbook at a later date, maybe after Harriet's death. The book wasn't the rich Moroccan leather of Lucy's, but heavy cardboard covered with black, leather-look cloth binding, probably from the Depression.

"Roger was born in 1915, so he was just twelve when his aunt died," Mrs. Timberlake explained. She stayed with me while I read the first clippings, but soon tired of how long I was taking and excused herself. She didn't come back till my stomach was rumbling and I knew it must be lunchtime. I hadn't looked up from the book in almost two hours.

There was the clipping I also had, of Harriet's stage debut. Or rather, her professional stage debut, because before that there had been starring roles in school and community productions, right up until she won the role in the local photoplay where she met Lucy. There was, in fact, a large ad from the *Saratogian* in 1917 announcing the opening of that film, called *Samantha at Saratoga,* from a nineteenth-century novel by the same name. "Introducing Saratoga's own, MISS HARRIET TIMBERLAKE," it broadcasted in bold capitals.

There were playbills from theaters up and down the East Coast for plays I'd never heard of by writers who had fallen into probably well-deserved obscurity. In a few instances, there were publicity pictures of the productions, and in fewer still, photographs of the leading players. They were so stilted and fuzzy, I hardly recognized Harriet. There was only one picture I knew well, because the original was in my scrapbook: a rakish profile, with Harriet smiling from beneath the brim of a cloche hat.

I had just moved into the most interesting part, the part of

Harriet I knew nothing about—the movies—when Mrs. Timberlake returned, burdened with a huge tray that held our lunch. I lied and said I wasn't hungry, but she could have heard my stomach from across the room.

"Well, I'll just leave it then," she said. "I know you haven't much time." Which was true, but she looked so lonely when she said it, I put the scrapbook aside and insisted she sit down.

I don't remember much of the lunchtime conversation. I'm not sure I even participated, or if I did, if my words made sense. Because somehow in my left ear, Harriet was quietly whispering, "Not a bad career, I'd say. So I never became Helen Mencken, or Marion Davies. Who remembers them now anyway? They're only known for the men in their lives, the Bogarts and Hearsts." I had to agree.

◆

Intermixed with clippings and playbills were the cards and letters Harriet sent to her nephew over the years (probably with the official notices of herself inside—how else could an adolescent boy in Saratoga get hold of papers from as far away as Bar Harbor and Atlantic City?). I marveled at how sincere and caring she was in the letters, yet with a trace of the coquette I'd known her to be.

June, 1925

Dearest Boy,

Yes, today your old auntie made her first appearance in a real movie! Isn't it thrilling?! I wish you could have been here to see it. I had to get up extra early, before the sun came up, to travel all the way out to Astoria, Queens, to the Famous Players/Lasky Studios there. Then there was makeup and costuming and hair styling and I don't know what else before they finally started shooting my scene at ten o'clock. I say "started shooting," because they shot and shot till we got it right. Sweetie, Auntie Harry flubbed her part a bit at first, walked left when I should have gone right, and knocked over part of the set. I thought I'd had it then, but they knew it was all nerves. Next time through, I did it perfectly—but someone else goofed! Didn't get home to Manhattan till later that evening. But sweetest one, I got the very best present for you—an autograph! I went right up to Clara Bow and said, Hey, you've gotta sign this for my buddy boy! And here it is, precious. Look for your auntie in *The Love Bandit* later this year.

All my love, sweetie,

Your loving Auntie,
Harry

Pasted next to the letter was a yellowed scrap of paper with Clara Bow's signature. Underneath, a clipping from the *Saratogian* advertised the one-day run of *The Love Bandit* on January 4, 1926, at the Broadway Theater. One day? I thought. Then I remembered from some long ago film history class that that's how Hollywood made a lot of its money in those days—in cheap productions that took a few weeks to film, and that were called "daily changes," a term that meant they played only one day in each town. It was not glamorous for the actors, and the plots were worse than many of the regional theater plays Harriet had appeared in. She had gone from bad to worse.

As the sunlight was fading, I began reading a sensational story of how an actress was suing a director because she had been hoisted into the air by a wire in a circus film and left to hang there while the director and rest of the crew went to lunch. The actress, it turned out, was none other than Harriet Timberlake. She had the director arrested and pressed charges of disorderly conduct. The letter that accompanied the clipping was half defiant, half sad.

Maybe this will hurt my movie career, but I can't let that horrible man get away with this. They just wouldn't do that sort of thing if I weren't a girl!

So, I smiled as the room began to get too dark to read, Harriet's consciousness got raised. Lucy's influence, I was sure. Suddenly the table lamp went on next to me, and I started. It was just Mrs. Timberlake, looking concerned, probably because she might have to feed me a third time.

"Mrs. Timberlake," I began bravely, "I know I have no right to ask and no real reason to hope, but is there any way you might consider selling this to me? Or at least letting me borrow it to photocopy?"

She took a deep breath and let it out slowly. "I've watched you looking at it," she sighed. "You've hardly budged from that spot all day. Harriet Timberlake must be important to you."

It sounded lame to say "She is," but it was the only thing I could think of.

"Then I'm sure my husband would have wanted you to have it." I couldn't believe she was saying the magic words. "He loved his aunt dearly and would have wanted someone to write something about her. My children don't know it exists. Besides, they'll have plenty to remind them of their father."

I made a mental note to send her a gift from the store when I got back. It was the least I could do, for giving me such a large piece of Harriet Timberlake.

♦

I finished reading the scrapbook sometime after midnight, as I had gotten back late from Saratoga. I closed it quietly and didn't open it again for a long time. But that night, I had horrible, vivid nightmares—people flying through the air, hitting trees with dull thumps, dead bodies scattered along the roadside as I drove the familiar route to Saratoga in sunlight so bright it seemed to cut through the windshield. I woke in a sweat, screaming out loud, just as my car was about to swerve into a tree at sixty miles per hour.

"No!" I was screaming in my sleep, but when I woke sitting up in bed, I was really crying, "Harriet, no!"

"It's all right, honey," she said soothingly. "It really

155

wasn't painful. I lost consciousness immediately." I thought I felt her pat my hand, but it may just have been the smooth sheet against my skin.

"Harriet," I whispered, "I didn't know."

"Lucy was the one who suffered," she said, her voice trailing off into the darkness. "It was like part of her died, too."

"I'm so sorry," I said, though it was unclear what I was sorry for. Because of a freak, accidental death that took place almost thirty years before I was born? Because I hadn't lived then, hadn't known her? Or because of my sudden, stomach-wrenching fear that, having read about and confronted Harriet's death, I would now lose her?

"Harriet," I said to the blackest corner of my bedroom, "I still need you. There are things I still don't know. You won't leave me yet, will you?"

But the only reply was some soft rain at the window and a faraway cry somewhere out on the street.

◆ 24 ◆

"For you," Catherine said with a big smile, plunking a large, flat paper bag onto the shop counter.

"What a gorgeous girl," Tuttie said, pinching Catherine's cheek as she walked over to see what she'd brought. "She brings you presents, and it's not your birthday and too early for Christmas."

"Well," Catherine said, blushing (or maybe the flush was just from Tuttie's pinching her), "it's not the most romantic present I've ever given."

"Quick," said Tuttie playfully, "what is the most romantic present you've ever given?"

"To Susan, or anyone?" Catherine asked with a sly grin.

Tuttie looked embarrassed and added quickly, "To this precious girl, of course."

Catherine and I looked at each other carefully, coming up with different answers.

"A dozen roses," I said. "Long-stemmed."

"No," said Catherine, putting her arm around Tuttie, "I think it has to be the crotchless underwear."

This time Tuttie and I both blushed, and Tuttie giggled, "Oh, you bad girl!" I pulled my present out of the bag.

It was a Ouija board, the classic kind from when I was a kid, with the image of a ghostly blue spectre on a jet black lid. Instantly, I felt a chill come over me at the memory of all the slumber parties where candles blew out and keys fell to the floor at the appropriate moment, just after someone had asked for a sign. Ouija boards were both the terror and the delight of

157

my youth, for while I always had trouble going to sleep afterward, the light of day made me realize it was just a game like Monopoly and Life.

"Isn't it great-looking?" Catherine said. "I never had one of my own. My mother thought you could conjure up evil spirits with things like this. I couldn't convince her it was just a game."

"I never had one either," I pointed out. "My mother thought it was a lot of crap."

"I got this," Catherine said, "because I remember reading that Ouija boards were popular in the 1920s, and I thought maybe your ladies might have used one."

"Maybe Harriet," I said skeptically, "but not Lucy, and the others I kind of doubt. They were so practical and academic."

"What did they do for fun?" Catherine asked, and I had to admit I didn't know. I had assumed traveling was a favorite pastime, but Elinor had dislodged that theory.

"My friend Marlene had one of these," Tuttie remarked. "That was back in the late twenties. I must have been twelve or so."

"Let's try it," Catherine grinned mischievously, as if we were all twelve again and our mothers were gone for the day.

"Here?" I asked. "What if we get a customer? Besides, you need atmosphere. Candles, a dark room, wind whistling through the trees, maybe a full moon."

Tuttie, at the thought of it, whispered, "Oh, my."

"Let's do it tonight then," Catherine persisted. "At Susan's. We'll take you home afterwards, Tuttie."

Tuttie smiled nervously, pleased at being included but probably uncertain about what we were going to do.

"If I can call up my sister, Miriam," she said finally. "She died five years ago."

"Sure," Catherine said, "whoever you want. We'll order in. It'll be like a slumber party. You can even stay over, Tuttie, if you want to."

"Oh, my," she said again and went back to dusting the books.

♦

There was no full moon that night, but the wind whistled obligingly through a window I left open a crack. We ordered in from a Middle Eastern restaurant, because Tuttie wanted to try stuffed grape leaves. She liked them less, it turned out, than the falafel she had also never tasted before.

"I like this," she said between bites. "I could get used to eating this. When you said it was called 'falafel,' I was worried it would be 'awful.'" She smiled impishly over her pita bread, and Catherine and I groaned at the bad pun.

When we finished, Catherine quickly cleared away the paper plates and crumbs and brought out some black candles she'd bought for the occasion at the card store around the corner. I'd tried to talk her out of them—I worried we were taking this too seriously—but she persisted and finally won. She stuck the candles into two shot glasses after dripping some wax into each.

"There, that should hold," she announced, setting them at opposite ends of the coffee table. "Unless the vind blows them out," she added, in her best Bela Lugosi voice. She came up behind me and poked me lightly in the ribs, and I jumped a little. "Nervous already, Suze?" she laughed.

"Oh, cut it out, Catherine," I said, sternly. "You'll scare Tuttie."

We turned the lights out and began, with Catherine's and Tuttie's fingers lightly on the pointer.

"What do we do?" Tuttie asked, her eyes big and black in the darkness. Catherine's face was shimmering in a way I hadn't noticed before. I had a sudden desire to call off the game, to reach over and kiss that glowing face.

"We ask questions," Catherine was saying, "or try to bring a spirit into the room. Like your sister. Want to start with that? We have to concentrate really hard."

So we did. Catherine, who remembered better than I just how the game worked, orchestrated the whole thing.

"We would like to call the spirit of Miriam Posner Feldstein to join us," she said solemnly, as if she were conducting a religious service. She paused, then continued, "Miriam, are you with us?"

I noticed a slight tremor in the pointer, but it was a false start. We waited a few minutes before Catherine repeated the request.

But the pointer remained firm.

"You're not pressing too hard, are you Tuttie?" I asked. "It should be a light touch."

Tuttie showed me that her fingers were barely touching the pointer.

"Try asking something else," I suggested. "Phrase the question differently."

"Miriam," Catherine said, "why won't you join us?"

Again, the pointer never budged. I was confused. It always worked when I was twelve. Did that mean someone was always cheating? I remembered calling up Janis Joplin, Jimi Hendrix, Robert Kennedy. They always spoke to us. It was like magic, cutting through time and mortality, and I didn't like having my childhood notion of the power of Ouija boards destroyed.

"Let's try just asking any old question," I suggested. "Forget Miriam for now. What would you like to know, Tuttie? Something about the future."

The party sobered as Tuttie, wise-cracking wit, asked the board, "How long will I live?"

We held our breath. Did we really want to know that? This time the pointer slid beneath their fingers and spelled out the simple word, "long."

"Well, good," Catherine said, with real relief. "We're glad to have you with us, spirit, whoever you are."

We continued the game for over an hour, learning things about our future that we accepted with great hope. Catherine and I would find an apartment downtown. I'd publish a book. The store would flourish. Tuttie would have another boyfriend. Still, we could not summon Tuttie's sister, because, our spirit told us, her essence was "too weak" matched against its own. Finally, the spirit seemed to be getting tired; it wasn't finishing words and some were garbled nonsense messages.

We decided to sign off. But before we did, Tuttie, now thoroughly entranced by the game, asked, "Will you tell us your name, you gorgeous ghost?"

The pointer hesitated, started to move toward "No," then gave us two initials instead.

"Who do you suppose it is?" Tuttie asked, because she wasn't as familiar as Catherine and I with my ghosts.

"My God," Catherine said, looking for the first time as if she really understood what I'd been through. "It's Lucy and Harriet."

In the bedroom, the wind through the window blew something off my dresser onto the floor.

♦

"So, when are you going to publish that book?" Catherine asked, out of left field. "And what's it going to be about?" We were situated on my living room floor, Lucy's cardboard box between us, papers strewn on either side of our legs. In our new, more open arrangement, I felt more comfortable sharing with Catherine. I had wanted a glass of wine for the work we were doing, but Catherine had prohibited food and drink from within ten feet of historical documents. "Now that you don't have to think about term papers, and the store is managing pretty well, you don't seem to have a good excuse not to write anymore."

"Shh," I said. "I can't concentrate," but mostly I didn't want to hear what she had to say. I had used all my schooling as an excuse not to write anything creative, yet I still called myself a writer. One day soon I'd have to stop doing that. After all, I had officially quit Columbia when my leave of absence drew to a close. Now I had time to write, and I still didn't. It was embarrassing when people asked, "Oh, and what are you writing?"

"A novel," I often lied, because the truth was I hadn't written a word of fiction in four years. "But it's too raw to talk about right now."

How I hated myself for saying things like that! I sounded

like every other pretentious writer I'd ever gotten bored with at cocktail parties. The truth was, it didn't sound any better to say, "I'm having this tremendous block. I haven't written in years. I'm afraid the well's gone dry."

But I did still think of myself as a writer. I had always thought of myself that way, as far back as I could remember. But the only time I'd been confident of my art, the only time I'd been prolific, was before I started college. For some reason, all the reams of stuff I'd written as a kid—poetry, fiction, essays—I boxed up before I went away to school and told my mother she could put it out with the trash. Luckily, my mother was smarter than that. Ten years later while visiting home, I wistfully remembered the time I threw all my childhood writing away. "What a dope," I said, sadly.

"You may be a dope, but your mother isn't," she said and led me to the closet where she kept the box all those years. I cried and promised her I would never again throw a piece of my writing away.

And I hadn't, because there had hardly been enough to consider throwing away. A couple of notebooks. When I first met Catherine, I was in the middle of this most recent block. She used to refuse to do anything with me on Sundays till I'd written something—a journal entry, a two-line poem, anything. She wouldn't even speak to me till I could show her something. Eventually, she gave in to my promises that I'd write later, after she'd gone. Then she stopped asking me about my writing all together. If I didn't take it seriously, why should she?

I pretended to be reading Lucy's journal, but my thoughts about writing were whizzing through my head.

"It's difficult to be a writer," someone said. "You have to spend so much time at it, alone." I looked up, and Lucy was addressing me from the kitchen counter. She was leaning there casually, inspecting my spice jars.

"That's the problem," I said, nodding.

"What's the problem?" Catherine asked, looking up from her stack of faded letters. "Lack of concentration?"

"Hmm," I answered, trying to sound thoughtful, but wondering where Lucy had gone. I excused myself and went into the bedroom.

She was there, of course, in a pool of moonlight, and I didn't turn the lamp on.

"You wrote so much," I marveled. "I saw the receipts from all your short stories. You had a lot of conviction."

"No," she contradicted, "just time on my hands while Harriet was pursuing her career. And the need to make money in the best way I knew how. Later, yes, that was more art."

I felt stunned by her honesty, like someone had pushed me backwards roughly and I couldn't keep my balance. In fact, that's the way Catherine found me, sitting on my ass in the darkness, in the middle of my bedroom. "I think I fainted or something," I explained, lamely, and she helped me up without questioning me further. "I must be hungry."

With a look of concern, she ordered in.

◆ 25 ◆

It was Lucy herself who gave me the idea. I have to admit I would have never come up with it, even though I had spent hours pouring over her personal papers. Catherine was still urging me to delve into history, do a slide show or exhibit, or write an article on Lucy and Harriet for one of the women's journals. And I still had little interest in that. Though I was learning bits and pieces of their lives, I hadn't strung them all together in an orderly, historical fashion. Both Lucy and Harriet were like messy, half-finished jigsaw puzzles, the grass and sky filled in, and the whole center of the picture missing. And I was still afraid what learning more would tell me—what I already half, or more than half, knew.

Maybe it would be better, I began to think, to write stories about them all—or a novel—to make up their lives as I imagined they might have been. I could change their names slightly, but borrow heavily from what I knew of their lives. Maybe that was what Lucy wanted from me, why she had chosen me to be the keeper of her words—a writer who needed subject matter and a reason to write again!

Well, I tried it. I sat in the evenings, on my day off, on my lunch hour, with a blank yellow legal pad in front of me. When that failed, I set up my electronic typewriter with a fresh ream of xerox paper next to it and stared hour after hour at the blank sheets I put into the roller. I bought a new daisy wheel for the typewriter so my words would come out sure and strong in Courier. I set a supply of black film ribbons by the desk. And after weeks in which I could not think of a single thing to say, I got understandably discouraged.

"Writing's like any other kind of exercise," Catherine remarked, wisely as ever. "If you don't keep it up, you get out of practice. You need to write everyday, anything, just to get the feel of it again."

How did she know about everything? I wondered, and started writing little bits and scraps of garbage everyday. It was all terrible. Still, I kept it. But when I sat down to start my novel, the pages in front of me were pitifully empty.

When two weeks had passed, I stopped sitting in front of the typewriter. Instead I stared at it from across the room. After another week, I put all the ribbons and paper away and unplugged the cord, the lifeline to my well-intentioned novel.

"I'm sorry, Lucy," I said sadly to the empty room. The feeling of failure sat like an undigested meal in my stomach. Maybe Catherine had been right to suggest an article or something scholarly. The creative drive seemed to have left me all together.

At one of my lowest moments, after a hard day by myself at the store on Tuttie's day off, I was sitting in front of the TV eating leftover pizza and watching back-to-back reruns of M·A·S·H in the dark, when I suddenly heard someone's soft sigh from the corner of the room. Dressed in a dark color, so I could hardly see her, was Lucy, bending over her own cardboard box and lifting things out of it.

"I know it's here somewhere," she was saying, busily, more to herself than to me. "I'm sure I packed it."

"Lucy," I whispered, so she'd know I was watching her and not the TV.

But she paid no attention to me and continued rooting through the box carefully, shifting journals and stacks of papers from one side to the other. At one point, I saw her fingering the fountain pen and I thought briefly, that's what she was after. But she laid it gently back in the box and lifted a flat brown envelope out instead.

"I knew it!" she smiled. "Here it is."

"What?" I asked, smiling myself at the absurdity of talking to a shadow. I talked as casually as if it were Catherine or Tuttie in the room, sorting through the box. "What were you looking for?"

In the time it took me to get up and switch off the TV set, Lucy had vanished. I turned on a lamp and looked for a trace of her, and there was a slight scent of lavender in the air near the box. I peered inside and found the envelope she'd been looking for laid carefully on top. I didn't recall seeing it before, and I'd been through the papers many times.

It wasn't marked, so I opened it slowly, like someone savoring the moment of opening a special gift. Inside was a typed outline and about twenty pages of manuscript on tissue-thin paper, with a cover page that said "Outline for Novel" by L.W. Weir, 1929.

I only had to read a few lines to know it was the novel I myself had been trying to write. Lucy hadn't even bothered to change their first names—maybe she meant to do it at a later time. But what happened? Why didn't she write it? Did she have a breakdown and couldn't go on? It was late, after midnight, but I sat down to read the outline carefully. Following it was a chapter of text. And as I was finishing, I heard a familiar voice say, "You go on from here."

"What?" I asked the thin air, but there was no clarification. "Where?" And it wasn't till the next day, after I'd slept with the envelope beside me on the bed, that I thought I knew what she'd meant. I couldn't start writing a novel about Lucy because she'd already started it. It remained for me to finish.

♦

"I don't know," Catherine said, and I found that hard to believe. I was sure she knew everything. Since our reconciliation, I'd been telling her every thought, every dream, every idea I had. It was just the opposite of the way I'd been with her before, the queen of concealment. I thought she was beginning to look a little worn down by my new revelatory manner.

Was it healthy for a relationship to tell your lover every little bit of inspiration that came upon you, even when it was something less than inspiring?

But this, I thought, this was truly inspired—by Lucy herself. "I don't know," Catherine repeated. "Has anyone ever done this sort of thing before?"

I couldn't think of any examples of someone writing someone else's novel, though there were examples of vaguely similar situations. The staged version of *The Mystery of Edwin Drood*, for example, where the audience picked the culprit. Great literature, important stories, shouldn't be left untold because the author died or disappeared prematurely.

"But that doesn't mean writing it," Catherine insisted. "I mean, it won't be the same, it'll lose its historical integrity. If you want to share Lucy and Harriet, I don't see why you won't just write an article about them. Something accurate. Or publish Lucy's journal."

"But that's not the whole story," I protested.

"You don't even know the whole story," Catherine said, a bit too sarcastically, I thought. "You still haven't read everything in the box. You keep finding things, like this outline. And you antagonized Elinor Devere, because she was disrupting your romantic view of Lucy and Harriet. Seems to me like you just want to make up the story, *your* story, the way you see it."

Harsh, but true. Who could read me better than Catherine?

"Honestly, Susan, you have to get these women out of your system or you're not going to have a normal life!" Her tone suddenly softened, as if she realized how severe she sounded. "I can see us now, in our seventies, sitting in this room with that decrepit box, saying, 'Which letter shall we read tonight, honey?'" She smiled at her own joke, and I laughed. "Promise me one thing," Catherine said after a pause.

"What's that?"

"Promise you'll get the whole story before you try to write it . . . in whatever form," she added hastily.

"It isn't all that happy," I said. "And I think it's going to get unhappier."

"Maybe," she said. "Maybe not. Just promise me you'll accept it." She was staring into my face intently, her lips set in a firm line, her forehead slightly wrinkled with concern. I wondered, for an instant, what she saw when she looked at me—some glimmer of promise, some molecule of hope? I looked so deeply into her eyes that I almost thought I saw a tiny reflection of myself in them. But she blinked, probably to break the intensity, and I sat back, away from her.

"All right," I said. "I promise."

◆ 26 ◆

All this time, since our reconciliation, Catherine and I had been looking for apartments. We decided we could even try for a co-op, since I had money now, and Catherine had saved a little. Neither one of us was very interested in the idea of buying, because prices were grossly inflated. But then, so were rents, and at least with a co-op, you got something for the small fortune you invested. During the hunt, our perspective got slightly skewed, so after a month we were almost thrilled to find a renovated one-bedroom for just over one hundred thousand.

"There's not enough room," I said sadly as we sat across a coffee shop booth from each other. "You know, that saleswoman had me believing that's what teeny-tiny apartments should cost."

"And I thought my place was small," Catherine sighed. "Honestly, we might have to give up this shacking up idea, Suze."

"Not on your life," I insisted. "It's too hard to live separately. I want you around."

She smiled. "You just want my body." Her knee rested seductively against mine, and the pressure of it sent a surge down to my crotch.

"You know me too well," I said weakly, concentrating on the heat between my legs.

"So what are we gonna do?" she asked.

"Go to your place?" I suggested, as a joke, knowing she'd

already switched from the topic of sex. She clicked her tongue.

"You know what I mean," she said. "It's a horrible situation. We just aren't doing what it takes. We should be getting up at the crack of dawn to get the *Voice* and read the apartment listings. We should be tacking notices up all over town. We should have a real estate agent. We should..."

I reached over and pushed two fingers gently to her lips. "Catherine," I said softly, "remember the Ouija board? We're going to get a place together. I know it. Things happen to me."

She didn't look the least bit convinced, but she finished her hot chocolate without another protest.

"There's a Clara Bow festival at Film Forum," I said. "I noticed it in the paper. Since we're down here anyway, let's go see what's playing."

"Who's Clara Bow?" she asked, and it was hard for me to believe there was something I knew about and Catherine didn't. When she found out it was from the 1920s, she decided it would be fun.

"Who knows?" she said. "Maybe Harriet will have a bit part!"

I knew that was highly unlikely. I'd read Roger Timberlake's scrapbook and I didn't remember any mention of Harriet in a Clara Bow movie.

Clara Bow was more popular than I had realized. We stood on line for thirty minutes to see her signature movie, *It*, complete with live piano accompaniment. Bow was beautiful. Both Catherine and I gasped at her first closeup. But then I gasped another time when Catherine did not. It was during a crowded restaurant scene, and I thought for a second that my eyes were playing tricks on me. But there was no mistaking her. Off in a far corner of the scene, wearing a shiny, feathered headdress and looking like she should have had a much larger part, was Harriet. The moment I recognized her, the scene shifted out of the restaurant.

I turned to Catherine, to see if she had noticed. She had

such a good eye for detail. She was munching a giant oatmeal cookie, lost in the movie.

Everyone around us was laughing. Catherine was laughing, too. She finally felt me looking at her and turned to offer me some cookie.

"What is it?" she whispered when I sat there staring into her eyes. "Susan?"

♦

I was right: there were no Clara Bow movies mentioned in Roger Timberlake's scrapbook about his aunt. I was certain if she had had even a crowd scene in one Harriet would have sent a notice to her nephew. Clara Bow was a star even before she made *It*. A part in one of her movies, no matter how small, would have been something to write home about. After all, Harriet had gotten Clara Bow's autograph for Roger two years before. I was confused but certain my eyes hadn't deceived me.

Maybe Harriet had the power to get right into the film if she wanted to. Like they had the power to become real to me and stand in my living room. Or visit me in Saratoga and have sex... well, I hoped that was just a fantasy, for the sake of my relationship with Catherine. Obviously, ghosts had abilities far beyond what mere mortals knew. Harriet may have decided she *should* have been in a Clara Bow movie and plopped herself into the middle of it.

"Are you sure it was her?" Catherine said, for the fifth time after I told her. She was thumbing through Roger Timberlake's scrapbook, reading bits and pieces that caught her attention. "Hey, did you see this? Harriet, the nascent feminist!"

"Yes, I did see it and yes, I did see her," I insisted. I sat next to Catherine and flipped to the last page in the scrapbook. Roger had carefully pasted in the obituary notices, along with a few dried red roses, maybe from the funeral. I read the one from the *Saratogian* again:

MISS TIMBERLAKE IN FATAL CRASH

Miss Harriet Timberlake, daughter of Mr. and Mrs. Wilton Timberlake of Union Avenue, suffered fatal injuries in a motorcycle crash on October 5.

Miss Timberlake, an actress who lived in New York City, was riding in the sidecar of Mr. Harry Baum's motorcycle when the crash occurred. Mr. Baum, also an actor, and Miss Timberlake had left the movie studio in Astoria, New York, where they worked, and were on their way to dinner with friends in Manhattan.

Near the studio, Mr. Baum lost control of the motorcycle and careened into a tree. He suffered a broken arm. Miss Timberlake received a blow to the head and died instantly.

Miss Timberlake, 29, graduated from Saratoga High School in 1915. In 1917, she appeared in her first photoplay, *Samantha of Saratoga*, filmed and produced locally. She went on to star in numerous regional theatre productions. Beginning in 1925, she was under contract with Famous Players/Lasky Studios in Astoria.

Funeral services will be held October 9 at 10 a.m., at the Grace Episcopal Church on Butler Street.

Miss Timberlake, who never married, is survived by her parents; her brother, Wilton III, his wife, Margaret, and son, Roger.

"She died in 1927," I said. "The movie was released in 1927. Maybe she never got a chance to make it!"

"It might have been made early in '27. Harriet died in October. You could check that," Catherine said determinedly. She took the scrapbook back and leafed through the end pages, looking for a clue. "What puzzles me is, who was Harry Baum?"

I didn't want to say it puzzled me, too, that it had been on my mind since I had first read the scrapbook and Evelyn Timberlake had mentioned Harriet seeing men. "Just a friend, probably," I said casually. "Another bit player."

"Hmm," Catherine muttered, unconvinced.

The puzzle over *It* sent me back to the copy of *Photoplay* Bea had given me, where I remembered seeing a publicity article. Sure enough, Catherine was right—*It* was made early enough for Harriet to have been in it, if indeed she was. So why didn't her clippings mention it?

We stayed up late, me reading letters from the box, looking for answers, Catherine correcting final exams. We'd both forgotten about our knees brushing in the coffee shop.

· 27 ·

Just after Christmas I had a call from Emily Fleck.

"Elinor is very ill," she said quickly, with her no-nonsense air. "She picked up a chill outdoors, and it's grown into pneumonia. She has some things she'd like to give you. Won't you stop in?"

"She didn't like me," I replied. "Our last meeting didn't go well, as you recall."

"Um, yes," Fleck said, faltering.

"She essentially threw me out."

"Yes," Fleck said again. "But she's reconsidered."

There was a long, awkward pause, in which I weighed what to do next. Say I'm very sorry and hang up? Or listen to Catherine's tiny voice in my head, telling me this was probably my last chance to get information from a first-hand source?

"When will I be able to see her?" I said.

"Can you come today?" she asked, urgently.

Tuttie managed the store in the afternoon while I traveled down to Grove Street. Unlike my other visits to Elinor, I had planned nothing to say or ask. And I had no idea what to expect.

Fleck showed me into the hallway, with which I was well acquainted. She looked more stern than usual. What, I wondered, happened to such a faithful companion when her employer died? But then, I guessed, Elinor would leave her well provided for; maybe she would even get the house.

Emily Fleck didn't seem to be worried about money,

though. "I'm concerned, I have to be honest, that you'll upset her," she said, biting on her lower lip. Her eyes were hollow with dark rings around them; she had probably been up the past few nights, listening for Elinor's breathing, administering to her needs. "She didn't want to go to a hospital, you see, so it's all fallen on me," she added as an explanation to something I hadn't asked. "If you upset her, I don't know what will happen." She was on the edge of panic, her voice just a hair's breadth from cracking.

"I promise not to upset her," I said, reaching out to pat her arm lightly. I *did* feel sorry for her. She'd been with Elinor for over twenty years, much of her adulthood. Like a married woman about to lose her spouse, or like Elinor when Sarah died, she must have been afraid of what came next.

We ascended the staircase to the second floor. "We moved her up here because it's warmer," Fleck explained. "Her bedroom is actually downstairs, so she doesn't have to manage those steps. She's in the guest room now, and believe me, she doesn't like it."

For one thing, it wasn't yellow, but a serious, somber blue. Elinor must have known it was a room to die in. She was completely covered; only her head, which looked tiny against the huge white pillows and puffy down quilt, was showing. She looked as white as the sheets, and for a moment I considered the possibility that she had already died. But as I approached the bed, I could hear her shallow breathing.

"Elinor," Fleck said softly, laying a hand on her hair. "Susan Van Dine has come to see you."

Her eyes didn't open till Fleck had repeated it. "We know you're quite tired, dear, so she won't stay long."

Fleck moved aside so I could place myself in Elinor's narrow range of vision. "You," Elinor said, and I smiled, thinking even on her deathbed, she was ready to confront me. "Lucy made me promise."

"Promise what?" I asked.

"Not to tell her family," she said through cracked lips.

"Tell them what?" I persisted, as gently as I could.

Elinor looked puzzled, as if she couldn't understand why I was asking these questions. In her mind, sick as she was, she must have been relating a much more elaborate story.

"I shouldn't say," she whispered. "You'll tell someone. I shouldn't say."

I took her hand and held it lightly. The fingers were cold, like the life was draining out of them.

"There's more than you know," she said, her eyes closing. "The nurse. Cervenak. Sophia Cervenak."

"What nurse? Whose nurse?" I asked, but her eyes were fully closed, and Fleck was pulling lightly at my sleeve.

"That's all you're going to get out of her," she said sternly. "For God's sake, the woman's dying."

But Fleck wasn't angry with me. In fact, she invited me to have tea with her downstairs. She was unaccustomed, she explained, to taking it alone.

"Do you know what all that meant?" I asked over my cup of Earl Grey. "Who's Sophia Cervenak? What's she got to do with anything?"

"Sounds familiar, but I can't place her," she said, sighing deeply. "All I know is there are some things she wants you to have."

We finished our tea quietly. I was really just a body to her, someone sipping and breathing across the tea tray, so she didn't have to be alone. I had the good sense not to ask any more. I had waited this long, and there was no reason why I couldn't wait a little longer.

When I got home that night, I looked up Sophia Cervenak in every phone book I had—Manhattan, Brooklyn, Queens. Lots of "Cervenaks," some with addresses, some without, but no Sophia. If I'd found the number, what would I have said anyway? "Elinor Devere mentioned you on her deathbed. Have you any idea why?"

No, that wasn't my style. Maybe I could coerce Catherine. I made a note of the name, so I could ask Bea Best about her later.

♦

Catherine and I attended the funeral service at St. Luke's-in-the-Fields near Elinor's house. It was our second funeral together in less than a year, and I was thinking how unusually lucky we were not to have lost anyone to AIDS. I had never been to a funeral with a lover before these two with Catherine. Weddings, yes. Graduations, too. Even a bar mitzvah in Queens and a divorce party on the Upper East Side. Funerals seemed to bond people closer in a weird way, in their understanding of the fragility of life.

The service was poorly attended. Elinor had few living friends and no relatives in this country. Most of the mourners were older women from the neighborhood, who also had brownstones and full-time companions. None of them went to the cemetery in Queens; it was bitterly cold that day, so it was just Fleck, Catherine, the minister, and I, plus the pallbearers, whom Fleck had paid for.

The ceremony was short and unmemorable, over almost as soon as we arrived. Elinor was buried next to Sarah, her companion of so many years. They'd bought the plots almost thirty years before, and Sarah had used hers first. I touched the cool stone where it said "Sarah Frances Stern," but then I caught the minister staring at me, so I stopped.

We went back into the city with Fleck in Elinor's car. I couldn't think of anything to say, but Catherine assumed control of the situation. The three of us were in the roomy back seat, me in the middle, and Catherine and Fleck talked around me while I watched the back of the driver's head.

"What will you do now?" Catherine asked.

"Stay on, I suppose," Fleck said, wearily. "She's left me the house and a bit of money. Most of the money goes to setting up a foundation to support people working in the peace movement."

"Oh," Catherine said, "that's so nice."

"I won't really have to work, but what else is there to do? I'm fifty-six years old, and I'm not ready to settle into my knitting."

"What about the foundation?" Catherine asked. "Couldn't you work there?"

"Oh, I can't imagine it," Fleck said, crinkling up her nose. "Me, in an office! I've never been anything but a personal secretary! I'd have to wear matching outfits and all, wouldn't I? No, that would never do." It was hard to imagine Fleck in pumps and a St. Laurie suit. Even for the funeral, her clothes were strangely haphazard. A straight black wool dress, probably from the early sixties, that had a number of unsightly snags. The ever-faithful Birkenstocks, presumably her only footwear, though there was a dusting of snow on the ground that made them inappropriate. And a huge tan trench coat, that hadn't been cleaned or pressed in a while, and couldn't possibly be keeping her warm. With a cigar, she would have made a good Columbo.

She invited us in for cakes and tea. There was quite an assortment of baked goods, sent by the neighborhood women, from the best patisseries in the Village. They were spread out over the kitchen counter, which was quite long, all unopened.

"I suppose I should do up a proper tea," said Fleck, half-heartedly, but we made her sit while we boiled water and set out some pastries. She was unaccustomed to being waited on, she said, but she let us do it anyway.

"I was with her such a long time," Fleck said sadly, nibbling at the edge of a cookie. "Came when Miss Stern was taken ill, and they needed help. I was just in my early thirties then, so long ago. She brought me from England, where I'd worked for the Viscount, her brother. She was my family here, really, like my mum." She looked helplessly around the kitchen, a large, well-equipped one. "What am I going to do here, all by myself?"

"You could sell it, and make a nice sum of money," I suggested. "Houses around here cost a fortune."

"Yes, and buy a smaller place," Catherine chimed in. "One where you wouldn't feel so alone."

"I'd have to get rid of all these things, too," she said wearily. "I was thinking of living downstairs and renting out the top. That would give me some income, too. But then you have to find renters, and who knows who you'll get stuck with?"

Catherine and I looked at each other over our teacups. My eyes were cautious, hers were eager.

"Susan and I are looking for a place," Catherine announced. I cleared my throat. Did we really want to live where Elinor Devere had died? Wasn't I haunted enough already? "If you go that route, we might be interested. We want to be downtown."

Fleck was visibly relieved. She took a big bite of almond cookie. "Well, yes, I'll keep it in mind."

After tea, she showed us to the office upstairs where the odds and ends of Elinor's personal mementos were kept. There wasn't much, mostly letters from friends and family in England, some souvenir items, a shoebox full of loose snapshots in no particular order. Fleck hadn't been through any of it and hoped that I would do that work for her.

"Oh, and one more thing," Fleck said, mysteriously disappearing into another room and reappearing with something clenched in her hand.

"This," she said, holding out the marcasite pin that had belonged to Lucy. "She said you'd want this."

♦

I have been toying with this idea for a while now. I think people see things more clearly when they're dying, that the act of leaving life helps them see the real meanings behind it. I believe this is what happened with Elinor Devere and why she had a change of heart about me. Maybe in her final moments she realized that her life would essentially be lost unless she made an effort to hand it over to someone, to have someone remember her. And perhaps not judging her life important enough to be of interest to a library or archive, she decided I was better than nothing. For this sudden burst of recognition, I have been able to forgive her her refusal to continue talking to me.

The letters from family and friends were interesting as documents of World War I. They were mostly patriotic drivel from the family in the Mother Country to their girl "doing her bit" in France. After reading them, I was sorry I'd never gotten to talk to her about the war, which was not the glorious crusade her parents believed it to be. What was it like for a lesbian? What was it like for a woman? What was it like for a human being? But I'd been too intent on one narrow line of questioning.

Elinor was not a writer, unfortunately, and there were no journals or stories to give glimpses of the past. Sarah's letters and manuscripts had all been sent, as Roz at the Archives had told us, to NYU, where they were still uncatalogued. Elinor had cherished only a few items: a souvenir program from *The Captive*, the lesbian play she'd told us about; a menu from a restaurant in the Village (some romantic connection, maybe?); articles by Sarah, most of which I'd seen in xerox form earlier, including a book review from *The Nation*. It was all rather interesting and unhelpful for my particular needs.

There were many photographs of Elinor and Sarah alone; most seemed to be after the twenties, because of their clothing and the decidedly middle-aged look about both of them. There were only three of The Gang, quite a contrast from Lucy's collection. One was a duplicate of a photo I had of all of them in Montauk; one was of the four in a slightly different pose, taken just seconds before or after the other. In the last, they'd switched positions: Lucy stood on the far right, next to Elinor, with Sarah next, Harriet's arm around her waist. Harriet was smiling at her, in an unmistakably flirtatious fashion. Why would Elinor save such a picture? Possibly, I thought, to dispel the image of Harriet that Lucy put forth, because Elinor thought she knew the *real* Harriet. Did she?

"Hold still now, ladies," said I, the photographer, as they shifted their positions, just for a change.

"We're always like this—Lucy, Harriet, Elinor, Sarah. Let's switch," Harriet suggested, choosing her spot at the end of the line and pulling Sarah toward her. "Now they won't know who's a couple," she giggled.

"Who won't know?" I asked, as I steadied the camera.

"Why, posterity, of course," she answered. "I don't know about the rest of you, but I plan to be known." She smiled at

Sarah and poked her playfully, but Sarah concentrated on the pose.

"Harriet, behave," she chastised her as the shutter clicked. And suddenly I was only holding a photograph of them, not taking one.

♦

The photograph sent me back to Lucy's journal. I reread the installments of romantic bliss, about Lucy and Harriet's first meetings, to buoy myself. But further on, past the writing essays, I found other entries, ones I could have sworn hadn't been there before, and as I read them I grew sad and disillusioned. It felt like someone had ripped my fantasy cleanly in half. Was there no perfect love? Did most romances crumble? How long did Catherine and I have left? We'd already weathered a bad period, but would we hold up in the next storm?

I fell asleep reading and rereading, and as she liked to do, Lucy came and tapped me gently to wake up.

"Why?" I asked her. "Why did you stand for it?"

"Why does Catherine stand for your antics?" she smiled. "Imagine, a grown woman seeing ghosts! Because she loves you, I dare say. And why do you put up with her bullying? Because you have something together other people can't see, don't want to see. Harriet gave me more than you could ever know, something others could never know." She looked me straight in the eye, something she hadn't done before. She always seemed to be looking off or past me, and I had guessed that that's what ghosts did. "That's what you feel from us. And that's what you have to communicate. What no one ever saw or knew."

"That," I smiled broadly, "is what I've felt all along! Why the facts didn't matter so much to me! It's something else, something... deeper," but as I finished, she had already evaporated into the shadows at the foot of the bed. I picked up the journal and began reading again.

◆ 28 ◆

October, 1930

The first time Harriet was unfaithful to me, I felt it like a hard knot in my throat. I knew before she ever told me. She went away to Provincetown for three weeks to star in a wretched play by the same man who wrote *Miss Morley*. You think someone would have stopped him after that fiasco, but he kept on writing plays and Harriet kept starring in them. It was August of 1920, and it was dreadfully hot in New York, but I only stayed in Provincetown with her for two days. We were having some difficulties with our finances, because we'd taken a bigger, more expensive apartment on Eighty-fifth Street, and I was making some extra money by writing stories and tutoring a dull rich girl. Harriet was making almost no money acting, and was spending it as quickly as she made it, so the burden of fiscal responsibility had fallen to me. I was seven years older than Harriet and expected to be more mature in all things, especially money matters.

So I left her in Provincetown, but not without noticing her rapport with one of her fellow actresses, Amelia Wingate, equally young, equally flirtatious, equally irresponsible. Watching them giggle together, I felt much older than thirty. I was almost relieved to go back to New York, to look up old acquaintances and friends I'd been neglecting since Harriet and I had set up housekeeping together. I was especially happy to renew my relationship with Sarah Stern, whom I'd met at Heterodoxy, and who was making a name for herself in certain downtown circles for writing she was doing on women and labor. I had not seen her much since I had wandered away from Heterodoxy, two years before, when Harriet and I became so deeply involved.

I invited her to lunch at Polly Halliday's, which was near her apartment and affordable to both of us (and, coincidentally, where Heterodoxy met). Sarah, I knew, was struggling, just getting by on articles she wrote for *The Nation*, and with a part-time research position for an economics professor at New York University. She could have been teaching herself, in fact, should have been, because she was brilliant and fascinating and full of insights into the history of the labor movement. But she was from a poor background, with no higher education, and she came by all her knowledge of the labor movement first hand. She worked for several years at the Triangle Shirtwaist Factory, till the fire there claimed the lives of several of her friends, including her companion at that time, an immigrant woman named Rachel Mikulsky. That incident, Sarah said, changed her life, and she has been active in different causes since that time. First it was labor, then that led her into the suffrage movement. The war in Europe made her a peace advocate. She tied all these strains together in a book she published called *An Economic History of American Women*.

She had some financial support also from Elinor Devere, her companion. Elinor was British, from a wealthy titled family. She had paid her way into the Volunteer Ambulance Corps during the war as a service to her country. She was one of the most dignified women I'd ever met, yet she was unpretentious about the station she had held in British society. She once showed me pictures of herself in France, during the war. One was taken clowning with a young man whom I had seen before. I asked his name.

"That's David," she said, "when he was touring the front."

"David," it turned out, was the familiar name of Prince Edward.

Sarah had met Elinor in France, where she too had volunteered as an ambulance driver. Sarah wanted to write a series of articles about the wastefulness of war. She had at first been hostile to Elinor because of her wealth and title. But the more they knew each other, the more Sarah became impressed with Elinor's quick mind and willingness to learn new ideas. They developed an odd teacher-student relationship, not unlike mine with Harriet—though ours was based more on age than on intellect.

So I was delighted to be spending time with Sarah and having a most enjoyable luncheon. She was, I think, relating an anecdote Crystal Eastman had told her, and was very near the punch line, when I felt something catch in my throat. Since I had finished my meal and was drinking coffee at the time, it took me by surprise. At first, I merely touched my throat lightly, smiling all the while and not letting on that something was not quite right. But soon the feeling swelled in my throat and I could not swallow. I began to lean forward and try to cough, and Sarah, by this time seeing my difficulty, patted me vigorously on the back. Soon the waiter and a small crowd of patrons had gathered around and I felt my face go hot and then cool. In less than a minute, I guess, the matter was over, and the waiter had brought me a large iced tea, gratis. The management, I suppose, was afraid of the adverse publicity of a woman choking in the middle of the restaurant.

It was a startling experience, because I had no idea what brought it on. The most startling thing was that at the time I was choking and having temperature flashes, the picture I saw most clearly in my mind was of Harriet kissing Amelia Wingate.

Very much later, when she returned from Provincetown, Harriet told me. I could have guessed by the look on her face when I met her at the train station. Because as she stepped off the train, as she saw me there, she averted her eyes for just a split-second. I knew immediately what it was that had choked me.

She did not wait long; she told me at dinner that night, a simple dinner I had prepared for her homecoming. Like our first dinner together, she hardly touched it.

"Something's bothering you," I said. "You're barely eating."

"I ate a bit on the train," she explained, but I didn't believe it. She had hardly looked at me during the entire meal. She pushed her plate away, but kept her fingers along the edge while she spoke. "But this was lovely of you, I don't deserve it."

"What nonsense," I said, "of course you do."

"No," she said, staring down at her fingers, pushing the plate ever so slightly further away. "No." Then after a long sigh, she blurted out, "I've been unfaithful to you, Lucy. I feel tremendously guilty about it, and it won't happen again."

I breathed deeply, evenly, enough air for both of us. I said nothing.

"It was a woman in the company, no one special, just a little flirtatious thing who complimented me day and night. I didn't even like her that much. I think I was just lonely for you," she ended, a bit pathetically, but in a voice so full of remorse it was hard not to cave in.

I, too, pushed my plate away slightly. I got up and brought the coffee that had been brewing in the kitchen. What she said did not surprise me; I'd known all along. It didn't even hurt very much. All of my hurt, I think, had been packed into that lump in my throat. I returned to the table, and she had started to cry, big tears that slid down her delicate cheeks.

"Say something," she demanded. "Anything."

I poured our coffee and sat down, reaching over for the hand that was clutching the fabric of her skirt. She started at my touch, then her fingers wrapped around mine, like a baby clutching her mother, the only person who stands between her and the world.

"It's all right, Harriet," I said. "I understand."

And I went on "understanding" for seven years.

Did I really, though? Did I really understand?

I have asked myself this question so many times, it has become second nature to me. Sometimes, in the middle of a lecture, when I am dissecting for my girls the meaning of, say, a passage from *Much Ado About Nothing*, the question appears to me as surely on the chalkboard as if I'd written it there with my own hand. And I find myself breaking off mid-sentence for what must be longer than a moment, because always, *always*, I'm brought back to the classroom by one of the girls asking, politely, "Miss Weir? Miss Weir, are you all right?" I stammer that I simply lost my train of thought, but their young faces always look out at me with concern.

How many times has this happened in the last three years? While Harriet was alive, I tried not to question. We had a special relationship. She gave up California—and possibly fame—for me. I remind myself of these things now, but still I wonder. I have to wonder why our relationship was not enough for her, why she had to find others. Why she even approached my friends, like Sarah. Are there some people who want too much of the world? And others who want too little?

Would we have stayed together? What was the glue that made us stick?

◆ 29 ◆

October, 1930

It has been three years, and the memory of it is as if it happened three days or three hours or three minutes ago. I had returned from a dinner engagement downtown with Helen Hull and Mabel Robinson. They had been trying to convince me that Harriet and I should take a summer place near them in Maine, and I was explaining that Harriet didn't share the romantic vision of country life. It was past nine o'clock, and I did not expect Harriet home till much later. They were finishing filming *Anything for Rosie*, one of those light little things in which Harriet often appeared. She was very excited about the part, because she had six lines, and her good friend, Harry Baum, played her sweetheart in the movie. They had to kiss briefly, and it was a bit strange for both of them, since Harry was of our persuasion as well. They were going to celebrate afterward at a rent party up on 136th Street. Harry was always getting invited to what Harriet described as "swell parties." I usually did not go. I was not much of a party-goer and thought Harriet and I should have some parts of our lives that were completely separate. Harry and Harriet often went out together down to the speakeasies in the fifties, up to Harlem, to Gladys Bentley's club or to the Apollo. Some people thought they were a couple, but if they had really known Harry Baum, they would have realized that was ridiculous. Harriet memorized all the details of their outings and told them to me later,

187

so I often felt I had met the people and seen the things she had.

That night, they didn't get to the party. Harry had a new motorcycle with a sidecar, and they decided to ride to the party in it, in appropriately wild style. He never said if he had been drinking, but he always carried a flask with him.

I never blamed him. He blamed himself enough. At nine thirty-five the telephone rang. Harriet always carried a little chit in her bag that said, "In Case Of Emergency, Please Contact Lucy Weir." She made me carry one with her name. She was always afraid if something happened, either one of us would not find out till too late.

They had tried me sooner, of course, but I was having dinner. I remembered then that at seven o'clock, I'd glanced at my watch for no particular reason, except to note the time. Then my throat felt very dry, and I drank several glasses of water in quick succession. And then I was myself again.

Harriet died around seven o'clock, instantly, they said, of a blow to the head that snapped her neck.

Of course, I blamed myself for the argument we had the year before. Harriet had been asked to go to Hollywood, to audition for the role of Clara Bow's roommate in *It*. Harriet worshipped Clara Bow and admired how she had risen from dire poverty to stardom, and she did not want to miss the opportunity. I thought it would mean the end of us. She would move to California, and I would be left on Eighty-fifth Street. She wanted me to come with her for the audition, and she swore that after that one movie, that one chance to play with Clara Bow, she would come back to New York to play in the legitimate theater. I insisted she had to choose: me or the film. So she chose. I suppose, ultimately, no matter what had happened between us, no matter how often or with whom Harriet had carried on, we were still best when we were together. She knew that. She stayed in New York and took bit parts in third-rate movies and went to Astoria every day. And one day she did not come home.

I know that I am not really to blame. Harriet would not blame me. She felt quite happy in New York, though when *It* was released, she could not bring herself to see it. I remember all of us, Harriet, Elinor, Sarah, and I, going to the premier of *The Captive*, and Harriet squeezed my arm and said, "Someday I'll be up there, like Helen Mencken, starring in a really fine play. You'll be so proud." I was already proud of her; and if I have one regret, it's that she didn't know.

♦

After that, it was hard to pull myself together. I went to pieces. I had lived so much with Harriet, as half of a couple, rather than as just myself, for so many years, I didn't know what to do next. Of course, we had had other friends and separate activities, but I had so much based my decisions on how they would affect the *two of us*, especially after Harriet gave up her California audition, that it seemed wrong somehow to have only myself to consider. Consequently, I could make no decisions at all for months. Choosing from a menu would send me into a panic. Deciding what to wear brought on an avalanche of tears. Not that I wasn't used to doing those things on my own, but without Harriet, there seemed no sense in doing them.

My friends, particularly Sarah, were very supportive, though Elinor said some horrible things that filtered through to me, as if it were no loss that Harriet was gone. Still, to see people we'd shared our lives with—Sarah, Helen Hull—was more than I could handle. I broke down completely one day, while dining with friends downtown, and had to leave New York altogether.

I went to Mother's house, back to Glens Falls, but Mother lectured me so long and hard about the temptations to evil facing single women that I stayed there barely two months, just enough time to put things into better perspective. Then I went back to New York and tried to made sense of my life.

For three years I have been unable to write. Every story idea has come to naught, the novel I outlined fell apart when I tried to write it. Distance, Helen Hull told me, that's what you need. Time to grieve fully. She suggested these journal entries so that I could remember the good and bad of Harriet and allow myself to miss her. But the distance isn't great enough, this apartment is too full of her. I have allowed myself to miss her, and I do. Oh, how I do.

◆ 30 ◆

Catherine was eager to live in Elinor Devere's house, but I was the one holding us back. Fleck had made the offer very attractive. She was already at work having the small kitchenette on the second floor expanded and remodeled. The idea of people she knew being her tenants had driven her to make the place as rentable as possible. The next time we went to see it, most of the furniture had been cleared out and sent to Out of Time to sell. The walls were newly painted a crisp white, and the room in which Elinor had died looked like any sunny guestroom. Catherine was pleading.

"Look, it's a good compromise for us, this neighborhood," she pointed out. "The west side for you, downtown for me. And we'll never be able to find this much room at this price anywhere in Manhattan."

We could have the entire second floor, a suite of nice-sized rooms, and eventually the third floor, too, if we wanted to renovate it. It was in disrepair and had been used mostly as storage space for twenty-five years. All at a rent less than our current combined rents. It was hard to pass up, and of course, we ultimately didn't.

I knew Lucy and Harriet would find me anywhere. But how would they feel, coming to Elinor's house, Elinor who had been so critical of Harriet? Would there be skirmishes between Elinor and Harriet that I'd be witness to, as the women fought through time and space? I wasn't really sure how those things worked.

I was sad to leave my neighborhood, so close to the shop

191

and to Tuttie's apartment. She was sad, too, and it felt to both of us like some sort of ending. The day before the move, Tuttie came to work carrying two bags, instead of her usual one. She handed one to me as she went to hang her raincoat in the back.

"What's this?" I asked. The bag was crumpled, like her lunch sack, but the bottom was flat, like a book. I pulled out a copy of a book about life after death and other supernatural phenomena. It was a battered copy that she had obviously bought on the street or at a second-hand bookstore.

"I got that from one of our competitors up Broadway," she explained. "Honey, their stuff's not half so nice as ours." She pulled out one of her spiral notebooks and flipped through the pages quickly. "Second Chance is the name. Don't waste your time going there, plumcake, we got them beat by a mile. But I saw this book and thought maybe you could learn something about ghosts. Or spirits, or whatever they're called." She thumbed through it till she found an interesting passage. "Here, listen." She read slowly and clearly. "'Some moment of the past has become totally real, as real as the present, and we realize it is as real as the present—or rather, that the present does not have some special status of super-reality, just because it happens to be here and now.' Funny, huh?"

I took it with a smile and reread the passage to myself.

"It's a, what's it called, a house-warming present," she said, with an odd little crack in her voice.

"We'll have you down for some Ouija board action just as soon as we're settled in," I promised. Catherine and I had begun to have Tuttie over for dinner about once a week, then would take her home, and I knew that's what Tuttie was thinking about. It had already crossed my mind a number of times. We would just have to fix up the guestroom right away, so Tuttie didn't feel like we'd abandoned her.

She was unusually quiet in the shop, not chatting about this and that, and when she left in the afternoon she simply said, "See you Sunday, darling." I thanked her again for the book and asked if she would write something in it.

"Oh my," she laughed. "I don't know what I'd say,

lambchop." But then she took a pen and scribbled something quickly and left with a faint flush to her cheeks. When she was gone, I opened the cover. "To my partner in crime," she had written, and I smiled, because it was the epigraph Sarah Stern had used, too, in her book. It seemed strangely appropriate, since Tuttie had become somehow a member of my own "gang."

♦

Sunday at work I found myself looking at Tuttie a lot, watching her putz around the store. Putzing, that was her word and one I thought she used to denigrate her own work. I considered the work she did for Out of Time valuable, but perhaps I didn't show my respect often enough. While she was busy rearranging the contents of the china cabinet to make way for some new items, I decided to tell her.

"You know, Tuttie, you've done a terrific job here," I said, taking her by surprise. She stood and looked at me with a Wedgewood box in one hand, a majolica vase in the other. She screwed up her nose.

"What are you talking about, sweetheart?" she asked, with an embarrassed laugh.

"It occurred to me that I don't tell you how much your good work has meant," I continued.

"You feeling okay?"

"Of course. Can't I tell you, as your employer, how much I appreciate the job you've done here?" I held the majolica vase for her as she slipped a few other pieces into place. She glanced at me over her shoulder.

"So, you laying me off, boss?" she asked warily.

"My God, Tuttie, you have to learn to take a compliment." I went back to the counter and pulled out some correspondence I had to answer. Tuttie followed me to the counter and set the vase down right in front of me.

"So, Susan, darling, what's wrong?" She almost never called me Susan. I could count the times on one hand. "You've been looking at me all day. I can feel it. Every time I look up, there you are, staring at me like you've got something on your mind. So what's the matter, sweetpea?" She laid a concerned hand on my wrist. "Really, you should tell me. I'm a financial burden, right? My memory loss is a problem?"

"Not at all," I said. "You're an asset, I told you. I'm just tired from the move." Her gesture was touching, and I put a hand over hers with a smile. "I'll be okay."

She seemed to be unconvinced, hesitating before she picked up the vase again. She stood looking at me, her brow furrowed with concern.

"If you ever want to hire a younger person, you just tell me," she said. "I can always work at McDonald's. They hire old people, you know." I couldn't believe my compliment had gotten so skewed. After she'd left for the day, I decided I should give her a raise to back up my words. I'd figure out how much and tell her the next day. But the next afternoon, when she was scheduled to work, Tuttie didn't show up.

◆ 31 ◆

I kept calling her apartment till closing time, but there was no answer. I left a frantic message for Catherine at school, but she called and said there must be a logical explanation. I didn't see how there could be. The facts were simple: Tuttie, the world's most responsible employee, who called if she were going to be five minutes late, hadn't come to work, hadn't called and wasn't answering her phone. Something had obviously happened to her. Even if she were still upset about the day before, she would have called or come in to discuss it. That was her style. This—this silence—could only mean trouble.

I closed the shop a little early, even though it had been moderately busy, and went to Tuttie's apartment to check on her. In the elevator, my heart was beating fast and loud. I had no idea what I would find at Tuttie's. My mind went back in time to the day I had come back from upstate to discover Margielove missing. If I'd lost Tuttie, too, I couldn't see how I'd face it. Maybe the shop was cursed in some way by a former owner or employee. Maybe nothing but evil could happen to people who worked there. Maybe I was doomed just like...

"Tuttie!" I shouted with relief when she answered my knock. "Tuttie!" It was all I could say. I threw my arms around her and hugged her till she protested.

"Susan, Susan, get a grip on yourself," she said, and I felt her hands on my chest, pushing me away. "What's the matter with you?"

"Tuttie, I was sure you were dead!" I was smiling while I

said it, which must have looked a little incongruous to her.

"So I guess you're glad I'm not?" she asked cautiously, closing the door behind me and padding into her living room in her terrycloth scuffs. She did not look like she had been home all day, ill. In fact, she looked like she had just gotten home from somewhere. She had on the blouse and skirt she often wore on Saturday, for dress, and her face was still made up. She had slipped her scuffs on over her nylons.

"Sorry I couldn't reach you today," she said, offering me a cup of coffee. "I left too early in the morning and just got back."

"From where?" I asked, now a little perturbed that I had worried all day for nothing.

"Long Island," she said, flopping onto the worn sofa and kicking off her slippers. "You don't have to pay me if you don't want to, but it was business."

I sat down next to her and drank my coffee. "Do you want to explain a little more?" I asked in a clipped voice.

"I got to thinking about how valuable you kept saying I was, but how I don't feel that way at all. I putz here, I putz there. I forget what I sold yesterday." She looked very sad. "I don't feel like I make a contribution. So I got to thinking, what can I do? Then I got an idea. Last night I called my second cousin Mildred in Westbury, she's hoarded a lot of stuff in her basement over the years, and I heard she's moving to Florida. I figured she'd want to lighten her load a little. I said, 'Millie, have I got a deal for you,' and I went out there and bought a lot of stuff for the store. Good things. Quality things. Some came from Germany with Uncle Sol. And I didn't cheat her, I think I paid a fair price. Wait'll you see the stuff, lambchop. It's quality."

I smiled weakly, still annoyed that she hadn't called, but my anger was fading fast. "Where is it?"

"Still at Millie's," she answered. "We just have to get it out. We have a few weeks. It's not too big, mostly china and linens and things like that. A few lamps. Some prints. A walnut desk."

"A desk!" I laughed. "Sounds pretty big to me. What else?

A sideboard? A breakfront? An organ?" I couldn't think of anything bigger than that.

She didn't laugh, as I'd expected. In fact, her head fell forward a little and she looked about ready to cry. "Go ahead, make fun of me. It wasn't an easy trip. I did it for you."

I could have kicked myself and would have, if my foot would have reached back there. Instead, I put my hand gently on her shoulder. "You did good, Tuttie. It sounds like great stuff. I'm sorry I laughed."

"Apology accepted," she said, more quickly than I imagined. "So, lambchop, I should apologize, too. I could have called. I just didn't. I was still a little confused about our talk. Thought it wouldn't hurt for you to worry."

"Well, I did," I said, smiling. "Don't do it again."

"You can fire me if you want to," a sly grin forming at one end of her mouth. "But without me, you'll never get Millie's stuff."

"Well, then," I played along, "I guess you've got me, haven't you? It looks like maybe I should give you a raise, to keep you around." I called Catherine to say I would be late, then took Tuttie out for a falafel sandwich.

◆

That was how Tuttie became the manager of Out of Time. It didn't occur to me that day, but the seed of the idea got planted then. It took me several more weeks to decide that what I really needed to do, for my own sanity, was to go into semi-retirement and write my book about Lucy. Or Lucy's book about herself, whatever the project turned into.

The day I went to Long Island, to Tuttie's cousin Millie to pick up what Tuttie had purchased, was the day that really clinched it for me. Tuttie had picked up some wonderful antiques for a fair price, and Millie's friends with bulging basements were now calling Tuttie every few days. I realized that Tuttie's taste in antiques was better than my own, better than Margielove's. Tuttie actually read up on things. With her direction, the store was destined to become a classier operation than I could have made it, and a far cry from the run-down junk shop Margielove had run. In a way, it made me sad. The junky aspect was what had brought me to the store in the first place. Without it, I would have walked by, maybe becoming a clerk in the Key Food up the block. I would be poor, out of school, probably out of my apartment, maybe out of a girlfriend. And I would have never made all those trips north to unravel Lucy's secrets. I like to think about what might have been. It makes me feel so lucky.

Now it was time for the shop to move on, out of the past and into the future that Tuttie was going to stake out for it. Tuttie would run the store, with the help of a part-time clerk; I would still keep the books, but I wouldn't be around on a daily basis. She might enlist my help and my station wagon to go on buying trips. But essentially, I was a free woman, for as long as I needed to be.

My last day of work was still one more ending. Now I wouldn't be living in Tuttie's neighborhood or seeing her daily, though we'd talk on the phone a lot. This time, though, Tuttie seemed less sad. She was embarking on something new, like a new relationship, when every day brings some thrilling new discovery. Ever since she'd disappeared to Long Island, Tuttie acted more confident of her knowledge and abilities. She even seemed to remember things better, but she said that was probably just my imagination. Maybe it was; maybe seeing her write in those little spiral notebooks became so second nature to me that I hardly noticed her doing it anymore. Whatever, I left the store that last day feeling confident about Tuttie and scared about what was facing me. When the next morning came, and I realized I had a whole day to myself, and endless more just like it, I panicked.

I woke up late and ate a big, long breakfast, which was unusual because I rarely ate before noon. I puttered around my desk, pushed it from one side of the room to the other, went out to buy a typewriter ribbon. Fleck wasn't home when I knocked on her door, so I proceeded crosstown to Catherine's school, where I waited in the admissions office for her class to end. Sitting on a stiff chair by the door, I got curious looks from teachers and students alike. I was too old to be a student, too young to be anyone's mother. I had forgotten to bring a book, so I read a pamphlet on drug and alcohol abuse and another on preparing for the SAT's.

Catherine walked right past me, did a double-take, then stood over me, as if I were a truant. "What are you doing here?" she asked in a hushed voice that made it clear this surprise had been a mistake.

"I thought we could have lunch. To celebrate my first day." I could tell from her raised eyebrows that she could see right through me. "I'm trying to be more spontaneous."

She looked over her shoulder to see who was listening and a lot of people were. The secretary behind the counter was watching us as she sorted through slips of paper of various sizes, probably parental excuses. Catherine hated public scenes. Her voice fell to a level I could barely make out.

"It's hard to be spontaneous in a high school," she said. Or that, at least, is what I heard. "You're using me to avoid your work. I won't be a part of that."

She turned around, walked to the counter, asked for her messages. There weren't any.

"I have to monitor a study hall now, then advise the History Club. I think you should go home and sit down at your desk. We can discuss this later."

I didn't like Catherine's teacher persona, and I wasn't about to make a scene that she'd hold against me for months. I don't think I said goodbye. On the street, I realized I was crying; but it was less because of Catherine's abruptness than because I knew I had to go home.

◆ 32 ◆

I made one more stop before heading back to Grove Street. The day was nothing like the one when I'd first wandered into Bea Best's antique shop, unaware that I was about to become a thief. The place looked different on a cold sunny day in March. It also looked as if Bea had shifted things around quite a bit. Sold them, probably, even though this shop didn't feel like a place where actual sales transactions occurred. It was more of a museum, a slice of time, with Bea thrown in to create a certain atmosphere. I noticed as I walked in that there was no longer a bell on the door.

Bea was dusting the bookshelves with a bright turquoise feather duster. It was the most colorful thing in the room. The bell had been replaced by an annoying squeaky hinge that signaled my entrance.

"Hello, Bea," I said.

"Oh, yes," she said. "Hello."

She didn't stop dusting, and for a moment I wondered if she remembered me. After all, we had only seen each other two times in the last year, and she probably saw a lot of brown-haired, thirtyish women of average height. But considering what I'd been through, how could she forget? I was starting to feel miffed, when she spoke from the bookshelves, her back toward me.

"I understand you've had a change of venue," she commented, flatly. I was surprised that she knew.

"Yes, it's quite nice," I replied. "How did you know?"

"I sent something to you, and it came back," she explained, but didn't offer to give it to me now.

"You won't believe this," I said, "but I'm living in Elinor Devere's house. She was one of your aunt's circle of friends."

She looked startled. "That's odd," she said, thoughtfully. "If you were going to do something like that, I would have expected you to pick Aunt Lucy's old apartment instead."

"I looked into that building, but there was nothing available then, and I was too poor anyway," I said. "I've had a change of fortune, too, you see."

"Yes, well, that would make a difference." She sounded incredibly bored, as she always had when she talked to me. I wondered if it was just I who bored her, or everyone. I realized I had never really seen her interact with anyone else. "And what is it you'd like from me today?"

Her bluntness was always disconcerting, and I stammered a bit, putting my thoughts together.

"N-nothing, really," I said, then knew that wasn't exactly true. "Well, honestly, I just wanted to tell you what I've been thinking about."

That came out all wrong, and she cocked an eyebrow, as if to say, why should I care what you're thinking about?

"What I mean is," I continued quickly, "I wanted to run an idea past you."

I was still standing at the door, but she had moved across the room and placed her duster on the jewelry counter. I wanted to suggest moving to the back room but couldn't get the words out.

"Would you like some lunch?" she asked, without changing her flat tone and without waiting for an answer. I followed her behind the curtain to her office.

Refreshments had been set out for two, like the last time I had arrived without notice.

"Were you expecting someone?" I asked, feeling disoriented as I always did here.

"It's lunch time," she commented, as if she were always expecting someone.

We sat on the humpback sofa in front of a tray of bite-sized cucumber sandwiches and glasses of lemonade. I ate three or four very quickly before I realized I had eaten anything at all.

"And now," she said, biting a sandwich very gingerly, almost as if she didn't like cucumber, "your idea."

"I think that Lucy Weir wants me to finish writing something for her."

Bea didn't look at me but continued concentrating on the taste of her sandwich. She finally put it down, unfinished, as one might in a restaurant and not at home. I thought for a moment she might try to send it back to the kitchen.

"I think she wants me to finish the novel she started writing about Harriet and her," I continued. "I think that she believes no one understood them and someone has to set things straight."

"More lemonade?" she asked, noticing I had finished mine.

"No," I said, somewhat rudely, and Bea looked at me in surprise. It came out much stronger than I intended, but I realized I wanted her attention.

"And you'd publish this under your name," she said, after a considerable pause.

"No," I replied, firmly, even though I hadn't thought about it. I backed down. "Not necessarily."

"Are you asking if I'd sue you if you published under my aunt's name?" she asked, as casually as she might have asked for the time.

"No," I said again, "that hadn't occurred to me."

"It should have," she said. "Even if I didn't, my sister Letty might, if she found out."

It was a more complicated issue than I'd imagined. All I wanted to do was please Lucy.

"That's a good point," I said, sadly. Letty hadn't actually threatened me but just didn't want anyone to be able to trace Lucy to her. "Though I don't know how she'd find out. Unless you told her."

"Yes, well," she said, finishing her lemonade and standing up. "I must go back to work, and I assume you do, too."

"I've taken some time off," I explained, finishing a fifth sandwich wedge quickly. "To work on this book."

I followed her back to the store, where she picked up her feather duster and resumed her work.

"One more question," I persisted. "Sophia Cervenak. Do you know who that is? What connection she might have to your aunt?"

She looked at me blankly, and I could tell she was honestly in the dark, not just concealing something. "I've never heard of her," she replied, turning away.

"Yes, well," I found myself saying. I headed for the door, unsure what to say or what had been said.

"You'll want that package on the counter," she said, without turning around. I hadn't noticed the package before, but there it was, wrapped up as neatly as all the others she'd given me, as neatly as Lucy wrapped her own manuscript. It was the package that had been returned in the mail. It felt like another scrapbook.

"Should I open it here?" I asked.

"If you like," she answered, flatly.

I ripped at the paper eagerly, revealing what I expected, a leather scrapbook. The pages were filled with postcards from around the world. Beneath them, in a childish scrawl, were the names of the places they had been sent from.

"To complete your collection," she said. "In case anything happens to me."

They were all from Lucy to young Beatrice during the 1930s. I was surprised, because Lucy's journals never mentioned travel. Yet she had apparently traveled around the world and back several times between 1930 and 1940.

"She traveled to forget," Bea said.

"And she couldn't?" I offered. Ten years of travel seemed to suggest that.

"I don't know," Bea replied. "She never came back. She disappeared. The postcards stopped, and she never came back." Her voice cracked in the first true show emotion I had heard from her.

"Are you sure you want to give them up?" I asked, suddenly saddened.

"They belong with the rest," she said, still facing the bookshelves.

I'd never felt anything for Bea before, no sympathy, no kindness. Yet, in that moment, I realized what a sad woman she was, how much she had loved and needed her aunt. I walked up behind her and put a hand gently on her shoulder, feeling it tremble slightly.

"Thank you, Bea," I said, and the magic of the store seemed to melt away in that one minute of contact. She was, after all, just a person. She glanced back at me, lifted a hand to mine on her shoulder, and patted it.

"You know, I never married, just like Aunt Lucy," she said softly, and somehow it didn't surprise me. It was the most touching coming out I had ever witnessed.

"Yes, I know that," I replied, and we stood there like that for a moment before a customer entered the store. We both cleared our throats awkwardly.

"Could we have lunch next week?" I asked, and she said simply, "Yes, well, that would be nice."

We began to have lunch then once a week after that.

♦ 33 ♦

The postcard collection added a new dimension to the whole project. This would be a novel about love and loss and remembrance. Lucy would head off into the sunset after Harriet's death and never return. Lesbians would eat it up. I'm not the only one, after all, with fantasies about true and perfect love.

I knocked on Fleck's door when I got home, ostensibly to show her the scrapbook, but more just to kill the rest of the afternoon. It was too late in the day to write, and wasn't it tea time at Fleck's? I still felt hungry from all the running around I had done and the light lunch Bea had offered. Fleck, I knew, always had some nice cookies and cakes.

But she still wasn't around. I found out later she had started consulting to Elinor's foundation, when she found out she didn't have to wear a suit to do it.

I mounted the steps to my apartment slowly, last thoughts of other stalling techniques shooting through my head. Go to the supermarket? Make dinner? Spend a few hours learning to prepare a chocolate mousse? Find other housewifely things to do?

Instead I sat down in the living room and leafed through the postcards. London. Copenhagen. Paris. Istanbul. Where had she gotten the money? The cards were spaced months, sometimes years apart. Maybe she worked her way around the world. It was hard to imagine how else she could have managed it on a teacher's salary.

The messages seemed to confirm that guess. From Paris: "I

start a new tutoring position on Monday. A rich American businessman's son, who seems to speak no French. If these people are to be found in Paris, it seems as if I will find them."

The postcards made me even more admiring of Lucy, if that was possible. There she was, middle-aged spinster, making her way around the globe like someone half her age. There were no references to Harriet. No comments about her former life in New York. No political observations. Just pleasant travelogue chitchat, the kind any aunt might write to any adolescent niece.

Even though the postcards weren't sad, what was written between the lines was. I found myself, by the time I got to the final one from Vienna just before the war, crying my eyes out. Was she very lonely? Did she ever have another love? What happened to her?

I went into the bathroom to splash water on my face before Catherine got home. In fact, she was late. I left a note for her in the living room and went up to the third floor, empty except for some stored cartons and the box full of Lucy's things. I sat down and started rooting through it again, looking for clues. But there were none. I'd been through the journals several times, but they were written in 1930, as an exercise in healing. Why did what came after not matter as much, even though she was probably witness to major upheavals in Europe and Asia?

"Lucy," I said aloud, "I can't believe you didn't write about your later life. I can't believe you had nothing to say about Hitler or Mussolini. I can't believe you let yourself die with Harriet."

"Oh," someone said, "no, you're right, of course." The Lucy who stood in the shadows was one I hardly recognized. She was older than the woman who haunted me before, with more grey in her hair, more stoop to her shoulders. "I always intended to publish what I wrote on my travels, I just never got around to it. Then I had to leave Europe quickly, when the war started, and a lot of it was abandoned anyway. But my relationship with Harriet—well, I took great care to preserve what I wrote about it. I left most of it at my sister's house, in case anything happened to me. Then..."

Did she really say these things? She'd never spoken so much to me before. Her presence was so slight, so faded, I could hardly see her mouth move.

"Then what? What happened to you?" I asked her, knowing full well she couldn't or wouldn't answer. Ghosts, I'd learned, don't give much away.

"Does it matter?" she asked, and I turned when I heard a door slam downstairs. Catherine, I thought. When I turned back, Lucy—quiet, thoughtful, middle-aged Lucy—had faded into the woodwork.

Catherine found me on the floor like that, staring off into the corner of the room. She must have thought I was working hard, because she never mentioned the incident at school. I told her I had decided to make an office for myself up here, instead of downstairs; and that, over the next few days, is precisely what I did.

◆

We turned the spare room downstairs into a makeshift guestroom and invited Tuttie over for Chinese takeout and a round with the Ouija board. I hadn't seen her in a week, and already she looked different to me. She had a new outfit on, a pants suit in a brilliant shade of green.

"Bought it with my raise, honeybunch," she said when I complimented her. "New shoes, too," and she stuck out one stylish black pump for me to admire. "Honey, I love my new job, but it just isn't the same without you."

"I know, it's better," I teased, and she smiled and poked me in the arm.

"What a kidder," she said. "So Catherine, how do you put up with such a kidder?"

We had all of Tuttie's favorites—Ta-chien chicken, prawns with black bean sauce, spring rolls, scallion pancakes. She talked nonstop about the store, which seemed like a different world to me now, even after so short a time. What would Margielove think of the way I had handled things? Would I ever really go back? My whole future, when I tried to think about it, seemed to be up for grabs, as clouded in mystery as Lucy's last decade.

". . . so I told him no deal," Tuttie was finishing as we cracked open our fortune cookies. "'Keep talking, success is near,'" she read from her slip of paper, laughing and crunching a piece of cookie.

"'Social and recreational activities should improve,'" Catherine read next. "I sure hope so. I could use some fun. I've done nothing but work for the longest time."

They waited for me. I can't explain it, but I had a sudden sense of foreboding when I broke that cookie, like it was going to say, "Life will end tomorrow." I cracked it clean in half, then straightened out the fortune.

I swear that what I saw there was "Ask the Ouija board," but when I couldn't speak, Tuttie pulled it out of my hands and read it aloud for me.

"Let's see what's made her speechless," she said. "'Make good use of time.'"

"How appropriate!" Catherine squealed. "I'm going to frame that for you. We'll hang it in your office!"

I took the paper from Tuttie and read it myself. "Make good use of time." Then I cleared away dinner without a word and set the Ouija board in the middle of the table.

♦

We still had the black candles from the last time we had indulged in this game. Black candles are really just like any other candles except for the way they make you feel—like you're indulging in something forbidden. In fact, one of the candles was worn down to a nub from the time a few weeks before when Catherine and I had sex in our newly assembled bed in our brand new apartment.

"Huh," Tuttie said, lighting both of them. "How'd this one get so small?"

Catherine looked at me lasciviously through the flames and winked. "Power failure," she said. "Remember the big rainstorm last week?"

Tuttie accepted that and settled herself with her fingertips grazing the top of the pointer. I was half thinking about the black candle, half pondering the fortune cookie incident.

"Come on," Tuttie said, sternly. "You have to concentrate. I can tell you're not concentrating."

She closed her eyes and started asking questions. We repeated the answers for her as the pointer skidded across the board. Clearly, she had come prepared with her own agenda for the Ouija board. Catherine and I were just her assistants, her eyes, for a full fifteen minutes, as Tuttie asked and got the answers to her queries about the store and its future, whether or not her building would go co-op, the fates of friends and relatives she hadn't seen in years. When she finally opened her eyes, they were clear and bright.

"Wow," she said, "that's really the way to do it. I felt like I was off somewhere, in a trance or something. Now you try."

We exchanged seats, but my aura was definitely not as strong as Tuttie's. I closed my eyes, I waited for the pointer to slip under my fingers, but nothing happened.

"Dumpling," Tuttie said, taking my chin firmly in her hand and turning my face. I opened my eyes and found I was staring directly into hers, which were two bright glints in the candlelight. "You're not concentrating. See how easy it was for me? You're not asking it what you really want to know. You're putzing around. There's something on your mind."

I'd never heard Tuttie so forceful. I glanced over at Catherine who was sitting stiffly in her chair, her long hands flatly on the table, like she had a feeling something was happening and she was afraid to know what. Slowly, I closed my eyes and called to the blackness behind my lids a shaky picture of Lucy, the one of her in the thirties, wearing the marcasite pin. I pressed my lids down tighter and tighter, forcing my face into a mass of creases and puckers. I concentrated as I have never concentrated on anything in my life.

"Lucy," I said, firmly, "are you there?"

The pointer pulsed under my fingertips and began its long slide across the board.

"Yes," Catherine read out in a small voice.

In my mind, Lucy's lips moved slowly in the photograph and formed the word "Yes." I had the urge to open my eyes and turn the whole table over. But I could feel the hushed, hollow breathing in the room—my own? Catherine's? Tuttie's? Lucy's?—and courageously, I went on.

I asked her questions about her travels, and she gave simple, one-word answers that often didn't make sense. When I asked, for example, why she didn't return, she said "Never," and if she ever had another lover, she replied simply, "Out."

"Ask her easier things," Catherine coaxed. "Maybe these are too difficult or require longer answers than she can handle."

"Lucy," I said, my hands feeling suddenly very tired, like someone had placed a weight on them, "did you die in 1940?"

The answer came quickly, "No."

I raced through the decades, trying to pin her down. At each one, the pointer would slide back then skid straight to "No." Cautiously, almost holding my breath, my fingers aching, I pressed on. "Did you die in the 1980s?"

There was a moment's hesitation, then the pointer took off for the opposite end of the board.

"Yes!" Catherine gasped, and Tuttie started breathing more heavily.

"What day?" I questioned, almost in a whisper.

Then the pointer ambled slowly from number to number, giving the month, day, and year, all in numbers. My thoughts made a sudden leap, as I realized that Lucy had lived to be almost a hundred.

"Sophia Cervenak, who was she?"

The pointer spelled out "nurse" slowly and steadily, but I already knew that. "Your nurse?" The answer came back "Yes."

"Where can I find her?" received the simple and unsatisfying reply "There."

And then when I added, ambitiously, "Lucy, how did you

die?" the pointer slid right off the board into my lap. I opened my eyes and stared at it.

Tuttie had started to cry, and Catherine looked as if she were about to. I had a terrible headache from scrunching up all the muscles in my face for what seemed like hours but was really only about ten minutes. Catherine went for the lights, and then stood behind me, massaging my neck and shoulders.

"I owe you an apology," she whispered.

"Why?" I asked, feeling the tightness give way under her hands.

"For not really believing you," she said. "It's been hard for me to accept that you see ghosts."

Tuttie was putting the game and the candles away, muttering to herself something in Yiddish I couldn't understand. She seemed to be more shaken than I.

"That date," Catherine said, her hands now caressing my shoulders, in a way that made me think we would probably have sex later. "Does that mean anything to you?"

I repeated the numbers several times. They had a familiar ring, but I couldn't place them. The most amazing thing was that it was only a year ago.

"Maybe that's when you took over the store," Tuttie suggested. "Wouldn't that be creepy?" But I knew when Margielove had died, and it was less than a year before.

It hit me later that night, when Tuttie was tucked away in the guestroom. Catherine and I were in bed, engaging in a little foreplay, like I knew we would. I don't know why it occurred to me then, when I was running my hands over her thighs, what the date might correspond to. Anyway, I stopped suddenly, turned on the light, and stared determinedly into Catherine's surprised face.

"What's wrong?" she asked, but I was already up and hunting through a box of my financial records in the closet. I must have looked possessed, because Catherine sounded worried.

"Honey, what is it?"

And there it was, the checkbook register from a year ago. I rifled quickly through the pages like a madwoman, till I got

211

to April, where I had crossed out a check for thirty-five dollars and marked in "never cashed." And, as I had known somehow deep in myself and forgotten, it bore the same date that the Ouija board had just supplied.

◆ 34 ◆

It had been almost a year since I'd stood at the entrance of the building on Eighty-fifth Street, trying to find out about vacant apartments. At the time, nothing had connected. But maybe you're smarter than I am. Maybe the minute I told you the super of Lucy's building said a woman had died, you knew it was Lucy. But how could it have been? She would have been close to a hundred. And why did her family think she was dead? Was it like Lucy to live as a recluse for almost fifty years?

I pushed the buzzer for 5A. The names "S. Cervenak" and "A. Godinez" were stripped in next to it. It took a few minutes, but a woman's voice finally answered. "Yes?" it crackled.

"Ms. Cervenak? My name is Susan Van Dine, and you don't know me but I've been doing research on Lucy Weir, and I'd just like to ask you a few questions."

There was silence, then more static. "Go away, before I call the police."

I swallowed hard and pushed again.

"I said *go away*," she yelled through the speaker.

"Please," I said, "I'm alone, I'm unarmed, I really am just a curious researcher. Please—just one minute of your time?"

"I'm calling the police now," came the crackling voice.

But she didn't. I knew she wouldn't. I couldn't possibly have sounded threatening. I waited there for a few moments, until a tall, striking woman in an oversized sweater and jeans came down to the lobby. She was not my image of a nurse or caretaker, though she certainly had the physical strength required. She looked at me curiously through the inner locked door and finally held it open for me.

"What did you say your name is?" she asked in a throaty voice.

"Susan Van Dine," I said, holding out my hand. She hesitated, then held out her own strong one to me. The nails were perfectly rounded, making my own bitten ones look pathetic. Her deep eyes held me as firmly as her hand.

"Sophia Cervenak," she said. She may have pulled me through the door, but I doubt it. It's more likely I followed her willingly. "Now what is it you want from me? You've got one minute."

She leaned against the wall in the lobby, her arms folded tightly across her chest, her eyes sizing me up. She had a good eight inches on me, and even if she hadn't been so self-assured, her height alone would have intimidated me. That, and the feeling I had that she was a lesbian.

"Well, I'm not sure exactly," I stammered. "It's kind of a long story. You see, a few years ago, I found this photo album that belonged to Lucy Weir. . ."

It took considerably longer than a minute to unveil my side of the story for her, but she was patient, unquestionably interested. All I wanted, I said, was to see the apartment briefly and to ask her a few questions about Lucy's old age. She never took her eyes off me. At the end, she simply asked, "You're a lesbian, aren't you?" and I nodded.

"Come on up," she said, and we took a silent elevator ride to the fifth floor.

I didn't recognize it immediately. I'd only really seen a few photographs. She led me down a long hall with three bedrooms leading off of it to the living room, which looked out onto Broadway through six magnificent windows. They were new windows, probably put in recently. The paint was fairly new, too, but the fixtures and molding had been maintained. The room was big enough to hold two sofas and a wild array of plants. There were various watercolor paintings on the walls, all in pastel hues. "My lover Ana's work," Sophia explained, when I admired them. "She's an artist."

It didn't look exactly like the photographs I'd seen, but it had a certain feel to it. It felt like Lucy had been here. It felt like a place at peace with itself.

"I can't believe I'm here," I said reverently. "This is where they *lived*."

She was still eyeing me curiously, wondering, I guess, what exactly I wanted and how much she should give. "You had some questions," she stated.

We sat in the living room, and I tried to recover my thoughts. There was so much in my head and heart at that moment.

"How long did you take care of Lucy?" I asked.

"Just two years, till her heart gave out. She had another companion before me, Martha, but she was in her sixties and she died, too," Sophia answered. She smiled, a bit roguishly. "*They* were lovers, *we* weren't."

I must have looked surprised. I'd never considered that they *might* have been, since Sophia was no older than I.

"I was under the impression," I continued, "that Lucy just disappeared in the forties. Her family had no contact with her after that time. Do you know anything about that? Why she lost touch with them?"

She seemed genuinely puzzled. "She never mentioned family."

This didn't seem to be going anywhere. Sophia hadn't been with her long, probably couldn't tell me anything worth knowing. I sighed, wondering what else to ask.

"But maybe there's something in her papers," she added, helpfully.

My ears pricked up, my heart beat a little faster. "Papers?" I whispered, my excitement practically taking my voice away.

Sophia stood up and escorted me down a shorter hall to the kitchen. Off the kitchen was a small room, which had once been a maid's room, and was now a catch-all full of boxes, painting supplies, a vacuum cleaner, a ladder and various tools. We wended our way to the back corner, where two medium-sized cardboard moving boxes, like the one I had with Lucy's writings in it, sat taped shut. "Lucy Weir, Papers" was written in heavy black magic marker on the sides.

"I've been lazy about this. I keep meaning to pack them off to Barnard, but haven't yet," Sophia explained, untaping one of the boxes for me. "That's where she talked about sending them at one time. It's journals and things like that. I should go through them, but I never have the time." She pulled a leather journal out and handed it to me. "I've gone back to school full time at City College. I never finished my B.A. Lucy left me a little money and got me on the lease here, so Ana and I can live pretty cheaply."

"What a nice thing to do," I murmured, remembering how Elinor had described Lucy as a caring person.

"Oh, she was special," Sophia said, with real emotion.

She opened the other box for me and brought out the first thing her hand touched. It looked like a ream of paper wrapped in brown paper. On the front, in the handwriting I recognized so well, it read "Our Time, Our Place." And beneath, "A Novel by Lucy Warner Weir."

"I can't believe this," I said, clutching it to me. It felt cold against my chest.

"Do you know about this?" she asked, lifting out some bundles of correspondence Lucy had received while she was abroad.

"Yes," I said, "I think I do." The air in the musty room had suddenly gotten lighter; there was a thin smell of something like fresh flowers.

"Well, then, maybe you can help with all of it," she said, replacing the letters and dusting off her hands. "It's not fair to Lucy to leave it here like this." She smiled warmly, no longer tentative toward me. She must have known that I, too, had cared for Lucy. "Say," she added, "want a beer?"

That was the beginning of our friendship. And the beginning of the end of my search.

Epilogue

Maybe I don't need to tell you the rest. Somehow, it all seems anti-climactic. Everything that had happened in the last year had just been leading up to that moment in Sophia's storage room, when I stood embracing that package and taking in the smell of Lucy. I didn't have to look at the wrapped manuscript to know it was Lucy's novel, the one she'd outlined and started to write about her and Harriet. Somehow, I just knew it. She didn't want me to write it, she just wanted me to find it. Why hadn't she published it? Time, maybe, or circumstance. Shyness, after all. Insecurity about its value or her talent. She probably wouldn't have known about the lesbian publishing houses that would have killed each other for such a find. In death, she realized it had to see the light of day and not be tucked away at Barnard. And she knew Sophia needed some help.

The box held a lot of secrets, and Sophia, Catherine, Bea and I went through it together. I took some pictures of us doing it, for posterity. Copies of all the magazines that published her stories were there, rare, almost delicate issues from the early 1920s. Manuscripts of stories she wrote in the 1940s and 1950s were arranged neatly in envelopes. There were several volumes of her journal documenting her travels through Europe and Asia in the thirties. Lucy had heard Hitler speak in Berlin; she was in Vienna when the Anschluss occurred. She had a brief affair with a Jewish woman in Amsterdam, whom she never heard from again, though she wrote of trying to locate her after the war. Her life was full and rich, not one of despair over Harriet. Clearly, someone had to publish the journals in book format and to gather together a collection of the short fiction. It was enough to occupy me for some time into the future.

When we came across the volume of Lucy's journal that revealed why she had lived out of touch with her family for so many years, Bea broke down. It hadn't made sense to me that Lucy had written off her devoted and budding lesbian niece. But it had happened that Lucy returned to New York just after the war began and tried to get her papers, photographs, and journals back from her sister in Glens Falls. In a fit of homophobia, Edith told Lucy that she had destroyed everything. In fact, I remembered Letty King telling me that her mother had wanted to get rid of Lucy's things, but that Bea had stopped her. A spiteful woman, Edith had never accepted her sister's life. Her daughter, Letty, had apparently taken after her in that. Furious with Edith, Lucy broke off contact with her but tried to keep in touch with Bea. Her letters to her niece, however, came back in the mail, presumably Edith's doing, but Lucy thought that Bea, too, had been turned against her. We found the letters in the box.

Bea held them to her chest and cried. She cried, I guessed, all the tears she had stored up for fifty years. She didn't read them in front of us but took them home with her and never shared their contents. We never asked. It was, we all thought, an invasion of their relationship.

"She told me she never came back," was all Bea ever said about the incident. "How could Mother lie to me like that?" I wondered if Edith had guessed that the niece was taking after the aunt.

Lucy had lived in New York all that time, writing her journals and stories and teaching English at a private girls' school on the West Side. There was also, of course, the magnum opus about her life with Harriet. She kept up her friendship with Sarah Stern until Sarah's death, and saw Elinor only sporadically after that, since in her later years, Lucy had severe arthritis, and didn't get out much. She'd asked them both not to reveal her whereabouts to her family.

218

Lucy had given up her Eighty-fifth Street apartment when she left for Europe, and when she returned, she found a place close by at Eighty-third and Amsterdam. When her old apartment became vacant in the early 1940s, she moved back and lived there until her death, first alone, then with her companion, Martha. Their relationship, though lengthy, clearly didn't have the fire of hers with Harriet. In describing Martha, she spoke of stability and strength and steadfastness. Was that what she wanted, I wondered, after the whirlwind of Harriet? Or could she not imagine trying to duplicate the sparks that had characterized their life together?

There were a few photographs of them together. Martha was a handsome woman, with an intelligent face, and unlike Harriet, she didn't try to dominate the pictures. There was something in the way she looked at Lucy that told me Lucy was the love of her life. How much had she known about Harriet? In the box, there was, after all, a framed photograph of Harriet, one Lucy probably kept out somewhere. It was as Lucy must have liked to remember her—not posing flirtatiously or clowning for the camera, but looking elegantly beautiful and happy on the platform of a train station. Coming home.

Lucy's writing continued into the early 1960s, and throughout, she remembered and made references to Harriet. Obviously, she had been as haunted as I had.

Of course, once I found Lucy's novel, wrote a literary introduction to go with it, and acquired a publisher, I was no longer haunted. My own creative writing block cracked, and I started a novel about the group Heterodoxy. Catherine helped with the research. Oh, on occasions, when I sat writing at my desk on the third floor, I felt something in the room, a sudden chill, even though the windows were closed, or heard a door creaking when no one else was around. But I never saw Lucy again. Harriet, too, had disappeared after I unraveled the circumstances of her death. I missed them. Sometimes I sat in the shadows of dusk, waiting for them, staring at their pictures, but they were gone. Their faces in the photographs were flat now, one-dimensional.

Then, a few days ago, I was sitting in my office, marking the galley proofs of Lucy's book and wondering which photograph we should use on the cover. I had the most likely candidates lined up in a row in front of me across the top of the desk, and I was able to narrow it down to my two favorites—one from the cliffs at Montauk, the other in front of the hotel at Saratoga. I was leaning toward the Montauk one, rather selfishly, because the Saratoga photo reminded me of my indiscretion with Harriet. I stared at the two for hours before I decided to leave the selection up to my friends. I would be seeing Bea for our weekly lunch the next day, and Tuttie had invited me to her apartment to meet Albert Rose, her new boyfriend. I would also run the pictures by Catherine and our dinner guests for the evening, Sophia, and her lover, Ana, who was as short as Sophia was tall, if you can imagine the pair of them.

After the four of us devoured the curried chicken Catherine made, I went upstairs to get the pictures. I was in a good mood, because I had had a few Indian beers, and we had been discussing a trip to Provincetown together. I was a little giddy at having a gang of my own. I practically ran up to the third floor. In fact, I tripped on the last step. Laughing at myself and out of breath, I switched on the light and went to my desk. And though no one had been in that room since I had left it four hours earlier, I could not find the Saratoga picture anywhere.

"Honey?" I heard Catherine call up the steps. "Suze, you okay up there?" She must have heard me stumble.

I took the Montauk picture and stared at it, and briefly, just briefly, I thought I felt the wind on the cliffs whip around my ankles. It took me by surprise, pushed me forward slightly, and I fell against my desk and back into the present. And there I was, standing in my office, alone, with a picture of four lesbians in my hand, and the faintest smell of the ocean in the air.

Paula Martinac has published two other novels, *Home Movies* (a Lambda Literary Award finalist) and *Chicken*. Her nonfiction books include *The Queerest Places: A National Guide to Gay and Lesbian Historic Sites* and *The Lesbian and Gay Book of Love and Marriage*, both alternate selections of the Quality Paperback Book Club. She has also published a young adult biography of k.d. lang. Her syndicated political commentary column, "Lesbian Notions," appears in lesbian and gay newspapers around the country. She lives in New York City, where she is working on a new novel.

Selected Titles from Seal Press

The Dyke and the Dybbuk by Ellen Galford. $12.95, 1-58005-012-3. A highly unorthodox tale of one London lesbian and her Jewish ghost. Winner of the Lambda Literary Award for Best Lesbian Humor.

Alma Rose by Edith Forbes. $12.95, 1-58005-011-5. This engaging novel, set in a small western town, tells the story of Pat Lloyd and her encounter with Alma Rose, a charming and vivacious trucker who rumbles off the highway and changes Pat's life forever.

Nowle's Passing by Edith Forbes. $12.00, 1-878067-99-0. A beautifully crafted novel about a woman who faces her exacting family legacy to discover her own life.

If You Had a Family by Barbara Wilson. $12.00, 1-878067-82-6. An unforgettable novel about a woman who struggles to come to terms with memories of her childhood and gains a greater understanding of what family is and can be.

Gaudí Afternoon by Barbara Wilson. $10.95, 0-931188-89-X. Amidst the dreamlike architecture of Gaudí's city, this high-spirited comic thriller introduces amateur sleuth Cassandra Reilly as she chases people of all genders and motives.

Nervous Conditions by Tsitsi Dangarembga. $12.00, 1-878067-77-X. A lyrical story of a Zimbabwean girl's coming-of-age and a compelling narrative of the devastating human loss involved in the colonization of one culture by another.

Working Parts by Lucy Jane Bledsoe. $12.00, 1-878067-94-X. An exceptional novel that taps the essence of friendship and the potential unleashed when we face our most intense fears. Winner of the American Library Association Gay, Lesbian & Bisexual Award for Literature.

Another America by Barbara Kingsolver. $12.00, 1-58005-004-2. A new edition of Barbara Kingsolver's luminous book of poetry, with six new poems and a new introduction. Also available in an unabridged audio edition read by the author, $12.95, 1-58005-009-3.

If you are unable to obtain a Seal Press title from a bookstore, or would like a free catalog of our books, please order from us directly by calling 1-800-754-0271. Visit our website at www.sealpress.com.